BAD BREAKUP

BILLIONAIRE'S CLUB BOOK 2

ELISE FABER

BAD BREAKUP
BY ELISE FABER
Newsletter sign-up

This is a work of fiction. Names, places, characters, and events are fictitious in every regard. Any similarities to actual events and persons, living or dead, are purely coincidental. Any trademarks, service marks, product names, or named features are assumed to be the property of their respective owners, and are used only for reference. There is no implied endorsement if any of these terms are used. Except for review purposes, the reproduction of this book in whole or part, electronically or mechanically, constitutes a copyright violation.

BILLIONAIRE'S CLUB

BILLIONAIRE'S CLUB CAST OF CHARACTERS

HEROES AND HEROINES:

Abigail Roberts (Bad Night Stand) — founding member of the Sextant, hates wine, loves crocheting

Jordan O'Keith (Bad Night Stand) — Heather's brother, former owner of RoboTech

Cecilia (CeCe) Thiele (Bad Breakup) — former nanny to Hunter, talented artist

Colin McGregor (Bad Breakup) — Scottish duke, owner of McGregor Enterprises

Heather O'Keith (Bad Husband) — CEO of RoboTech, Jordan's sister

Clay Steele (Bad Husband) — Heather's business rival, CEO of Steele Technologies

Kay (Bad Date) — romance writer, hates to be stood up

Garret Williams (Bad Date) — former rugby player

Rachel Morris (Bad Hookup) — Heather's assistant, superpowers include being ultra-organized

Sebastian (Bas) Scott (Bad Hookup) — Devon Scott's brother, Clay's assistant

Rebecca (Bec) Darden (Bad Divorce) — kickass lawyer, New York roots

Luke Pearson (Bad Divorce) — Southern gentleman, CEO Pearson Energies

Seraphina Delgado (Bad Fiancé) — romantic to the core, looks like a bombshell, but even prettier on the inside

Tate Connor (Bad Fiancé) — tech genius, scared to be burned by love

Lorelai (Bad Text) — drunk texts don't make her happy

Logan Smith (Bad Text) — former military, sometimes drunk texts are for the best

Kelsey Scott (Bad Boyfriend) — Bas and Devon's sister, engineer at RoboTech, brilliant

Tanner Pearson (Bad Boyfriend) — Bas and Devon's childhood friend, photographer

Trix Donovan (Bad Blind Date) — Heather's sister, Jordan's half-sister, nurse who worked in war zones, poverty-stricken areas, and abroad for almost a decade

Jet Hansen (Bad Blind Date) — a doctor Trix worked with

Molly Miller (Bad Wedding) — owner of Molly's, a kickass bakery in San Francisco

Jackson Davis (Bad Wedding) — Molly's ex-fiancé

Kate McLeod (Bad Engagement) — Kelsey's college friend, advertiser extraordinaire, loves purple and Hermione Granger

Jaime Huntingon (Bad Engagement) — vet, does excellent man-bun

Heidi Greene (Bad Bridesmaid) — science, organization, and *Twilight* nerd

Brad Huntington (Bad Bridesmaid) — travel junkie, dreamy hazel eyes, hidden sweet side

Ben Bradford (Bad Swipe) — quiet, brooding, had a thing for golden retrievers

Stef McKay (Bad Swipe) — lab assistant, dog lover, klutzy to the extreme
Tammy Huntington (Bad Girlfriend) — allergic to relationships
Fletcher King (Bad Girlfriend) — has a thing for smart, sassy women

Additional Characters:

George O'Keith — Jordan's dad
Hunter O'Keith — Jordan's nephew
Bridget McGregor — Colin's mom
Lena McGregor — Colin's sister
Bobby Donovan — Heather's half and Trix's full brother
Frances and Sugar Delgado — Sera's parents
Devon Scott — Kels and Bas's brother
Becca Scott — Kels and Bas's sister in law
Heidi Greene — Kels' friend since college
Cora Hutchins — Kels' friend since childhood
Fred — the bestest golden retriever in the world*Sir Fuzzy McFeatherston aka The Fuzz* — Jaime and Kate's pet rooster

ONE

Cecilia

CECILIA SAT ON THE PLANE, her first-class seat luxurious and insanely comfortable. It might have been the first time in her limited travel experience that she didn't feel like cattle shoved into the back of a truck, and instead, like an actual person with wants and needs.

"Your champagne, Ms. Thiele."

"Thank you," she said and took a sip, leaning back into the butter-soft leather with a sigh.

She'd just closed her eyes when someone sat down in the empty seat next to her.

Rustling accompanied the movement as the person got settled.

"Can I get you anything?" the flight attendant asked.

"A whiskey."

Every hair stood up on Cecilia's neck. Oh, *God* no. It couldn't possibly be—

She clenched her lids tightly, refusing, absolutely refusing to open them. No. She was imagining things. It had been years since she'd heard that voice.

Too many years.

"Here you go, Mr. McGregor."

Oh, fuck.

Her eyes flew open, but she didn't move her head. She couldn't chance it. But she did risk a peek out of the corner of her eye, and that was enough to have dread twisting her stomach into knots.

No. It couldn't be.

She'd booked this flight last minute, deciding to use the voucher gifted to her by Abby—her friend and employer—after she and her husband, Jordan, had returned from their honeymoon.

Cecilia's life had felt stagnant.

She'd needed to get away, and she'd had the free flight and hotel.

It made sense to use it, however last minute.

Plus, everything had worked out. There had been one first-class seat open. Only one cabin at her dream resort.

And now she was sitting next to Colin McGregor.

"Flight attendants, arm the doors," the pilot's voice chimed through the plane's speakers.

A *thud* signaled the disappearance of her last avenue of escape.

She was trapped on a nonstop flight for twelve hours.

With the man who'd left her at the altar.

How was this possibly her life?

"Cecilia?" that masculine voice asked. "Is it really you?"

And just like all the times before, her eyes were drawn to him. She'd never been able to ignore him. Not Colin. Not even when he'd—

But this time was different.

She wasn't weak. She wasn't a vulnerable girl in a rough place.

She'd been through Hell and back.

Colin had no power over her.

Not anymore.

Cecilia put in her earbuds and turned her back on the man who'd devastated her world six years before.

TWO

Cecilia

SHE WAS GOING TO YELL "BOMB!" on an airplane.

She *had* to.

It was the only way to get the plane to turn around, for CeCe to find an escape route from the awful man sitting next to her. He'd been staring at her for three hours twenty-two minutes and forty-six seconds. Forty-seven. Forty-eight—

Okay. The precise timing wasn't important.

But the heavy weight of his gaze was smothering her, a stifling cloud that threatened to drive her insane. And it was exacerbated by his smell, all spicy and male. It floated around her, making her toes curl.

He was the same as before.

As in, he had *exactly* the same effect on her body—an accelerated pulse, sweaty palms, a tense quivering abdomen, and heat between her thighs.

She wanted him.

Despite it having been six years since she'd seen him. Despite what he had done.

Cecilia's body still wanted Colin's with a longing that was so intense it was almost scary.

Her lady bits wanted her to tug him up from his seat by the tie—a new addition, as she'd never seen the man in a suit—drag him up the aisle, and lock him in the ridiculously small bathroom to have her merry way with him.

Hence, the bomb threat.

Which, obviously, she couldn't make.

It might be torture sitting next to Colin, but there were three hundred other people on this airplane, all with places to be, people to visit, sights to see. She couldn't ruin that for them.

Not that Colin McGregor would care he was ruining it for *her*. He crushed dreams, smashed hearts, tore tender emotions to shreds.

He was her Godzilla, and she was the decimated city.

Had been the decimated city.

But now she was rebuilt. She was stronger, her heart reinforced with rebar and steel, and she didn't give one damn for Colin McGregor.

If only she could convince her body of that fact.

Damns to give or not, she still didn't want him within arm's reach and so, shortly after takeoff, she'd risen and discreetly asked the flight attendant if there was any way she could switch seats, only to receive a regretful glance and an apology as the flight was completely full and all the first-class seats were occupied by couples or families traveling together.

She'd even started to ask about moving back to economy, thinking to make someone's day by offering them a seat by the gorgeous Scot, but the flight attendant had looked so harried that Cecilia had relented.

She knew they had a job to do and that she was getting in the way of it, and while she didn't want to be a pain in the ass, her current situation was truly untenable.

"You're even more beautiful than I remember," he said, and the rough edges of his accent hacked at the words, making them more of a growl rather than a soft sentiment.

Her breath caught, and she found her eyes drawn to the stormy blue of Colin's.

And she stared again, utterly entranced before she remembered how it had all ended.

Her in a white dress.

Alone, except for the priest, who'd given her a pitying look and invited her to stay as long as she needed.

But it had always been like this, Colin's gruff words winning her over. They were unexpected from him—he was typically so reserved and taciturn. And that compliment, freely given as it was, chipped away at any defenses she had managed to erect.

The problem was that his words weren't always followed up by action. In fact, they were typically trailed by pain for her and fury for him.

The hurt of those memories—of Colin so angry, her so broken—helped shore up her resolve.

"Don't say things like that," she snapped and started to pop her earbuds back in. Her friends at home had filled her phone with a slew of romantic audiobooks, and she decided that she much preferred fictional heroes at the moment.

At least if they broke their heroine's heart, it was only once.

Colin had already broken hers twice.

She wasn't looking for a round three.

But before she had the chance to insert the earbud, his fingers gripped her wrist. "Don't ignore me," Colin said, all high-and-mighty, all arrogant, rich Scottish duke.

Well, she wasn't a little girl anymore, wasn't a fresh-faced recent high school graduate taking a summer trip, wasn't even a slightly disillusioned college dropout. *No.* She was more experienced, and at twenty-six, she knew she'd had enough of wealthy, powerful men.

"You don't belong here."

"If you were worth anything at all, your parents wouldn't have disowned you."

The memory of Colin's words were bullets, stealing her breath as they shot forward in her mind to strike home.

She'd been so naïve, so stupid, so . . . completely in love.

And he'd destroyed her.

Twice.

What was the saying? Fool her once and shame on him, but fool her twice and shame on her?

Yeah. *That.*

Shame on her. For being a fucking idiot. For putting herself out there. For being a glutton for punishment.

"Let me go, Colin," she said, yanking at her wrist until he was either forced to release her or make a scene. He chose to let go. Of course, he did. Because McGregors didn't make scenes. They functioned in the background, skulking, stalking, waiting for the moment their prey faltered and they could pounce.

And to show her that he was still in control, that he was stronger than her and was only loosening his grip because *he* wanted to, Colin did it slowly, sliding fingertip by fingertip free, dragging them across her skin and raising goose bumps in their wake.

"I already did that once," he said, putting his arm back onto his armrest. A lock of jet-black hair fell across his forehead as he leaned in to meet her eyes. "And it was the biggest mistake of my life."

"Twice," she whispered, her throat tight, her heart pounding. There was an invitation in his gaze. He would accept her. She could crawl into his arms, get lost in an embrace that once upon a time had protected her from anything bad in the universe.

Except with Colin, that peaceful, sheltered feeling never *actually* lasted.

His expression clouded and she might have said he looked confused. But Colin was never anything less than one hundred percent completely sure of himself.

That was why he'd broken her so completely the second time.

So, she ignored the invitation in his eyes, turned her back on him again, and tried to pretend that she didn't feel like crying.

Her once-in-a-lifetime adventure was off to a brilliant start.

THREE

Colin

SHE STILL SMELLED of vanilla and jasmine. Her head still fit perfectly under his chin.

Colin inhaled deeply, knowing that if someone caught him, he'd end up looking like a bloody idiot. It was worth it anyway. Cecilia's scent hit him right in the gut, unfurling in his stomach and spreading through his limbs.

It smelled like home and also like his biggest regret.

She sighed in her sleep, turning over and nuzzling close, and her hair tickled his nose, just like it used to. God damn, did that make his heart ache.

And now, she was in his arms again.

What was the American expression? A summer fling? They'd had two of them. Except, it hadn't just been a fling for him. Not *either* time.

He'd given her a ring.

Had actually been heading to the altar when he'd discovered she'd run off with his best friend.

He'd been hurt and too angry for answers at the time. Then

later, when that fury had finally calmed enough that he'd wanted those answers, his family had imploded, and he hadn't been able to spare a moment for his idiotic emotional needs.

A month after CeCe had left him, his father had dropped dead, apoplectically screaming at a tenant for some perceived slight. And while Colin wasn't terribly sad to see the old bastard go, he *had* been nearly sunk by the responsibilities of inheriting the multitude of McGregor estates and businesses. He'd needed to dive in, to streamline because the family was bleeding money and would have been out on their asses if he hadn't taken the time to learn every detail of each of the companies before deciding which to sell and which to keep. It had taken years before he'd been able to breathe freely, but he was there.

And the deal with RoboTech further ensured that.

The McGregor coffers were secure. His family was safe. And . . . now what?

Or at least, that was what he'd *been* thinking before he'd sat down next to Cecilia on the plane.

Now, his focus was clear and revolved around a certain waifish redhead with piercing green eyes.

Though he supposed waifish wasn't the right term for her, not any longer. Six years ago, she'd still been a girl. Today, Colin found himself holding a woman, still slender and petite, but full of curves that his hands itched to cup.

She sighed and shifted in the circle of his arms, and he knew that it wouldn't be much longer before she woke. She'd slipped off about forty-five minutes after deliberately trying to ignore him again, but though her mind might be in favor of rejecting any interaction with him, her body seemed to have a different tack. As sleep had swept through her, she'd slumped against him, first her back then her shoulders and head, and then nearly all of her when he'd slid an arm around her to shift her into a more comfortable position.

Her head was tucked just beneath his chin, one arm wrapped around his waist, the other dangling between them and resting on the outside of his thigh.

Thank God it was on the *outside*, otherwise he might have embarrassed himself.

She shifted again, and Colin took one more inhale, knowing that she would hate both him and herself when she woke and found them tangled together.

The cabin lights flicked on, and CeCe breathed out slowly. She inhaled, and he felt her breath catch through the cotton of his shirt. Her back went stiff, her hand at his waist curled into a fist.

It was obvious the moment she was fully awake. Mainly because the second she was, Cecilia did her best impression of a cat being wrangled for a visit with the vet. She clawed at his chest, trying to shove herself back into her own seat, and in the process managed to both nearly unman him and catch a chunk of her hair on the buttons of his shirt.

"Jesus, woman," he ground out, grabbing her hips to steady her flailing movements. She struggled, her elbow connecting with his midsection and then *lower*. Okay, that was enough. He pinned her against him, trapping those dangerous limbs between them. "I'd like to keep that part. Just hold still."

"Let me go," she snapped.

"Certainly," he replied. "Or at least I will, once you've released yourself from my shirt."

Finally, she stopped fighting him. "What?"

"Your hair is stuck . . ."

Fingers came up to feel her scalp, and she winced when she found the tangle. "Oh."

"If you'll allow me"—she snorted, and he ignored it—"I'll release you." But despite the tension in her frame, CeCe didn't move as he gently worked the locks free. "There," he eventually said, smoothing a hand down her head and tucking an errant strand behind her ear.

She lurched off him and back into her own seat. "Thanks," she muttered and swept her hair up into some sort of intricate twist that exposed the back of her neck—

His heart stopped.

He reached across the armrest and gripped both of her arms, fury suddenly filling every cell in his body. "What have you done?"

Where once there had been soft red tendrils, curls he'd loved twisting around his finger as he'd trailed kisses down her nape, now there was nothing but shorn locks, so short that he could see—

CeCe frowned. "It's been six years. I cut my hair. Big deal."

"Not the haircut," he gritted out. "*That* I like. It suits you." And it did. The bigger question was, "Why the fuck do you have another man's name tattooed on your neck?"

FOUR

Cecilia

SHE FROZE at Colin's question, struggling to comprehend, her brain still foggy from sleep.

No. Her brain was a mess because she'd woken up in Colin's arms.

"*Cecilia*," he said, and her fingers drifted up to the name tattooed just beneath her hairline.

She was unused to people noticing it, since she usually wore her hair down or in a low ponytail, but she'd just gotten her hair cut and liked the feel of the air hitting her scalp where the stylist had used clippers to trim it short. There was something about the way it felt . . .

Free.

She rolled her eyes.

Or so she'd thought.

Cue her sitting next to the man who'd broken her heart.

"Who's Hunter?" Colin snapped, dropping his hands from her arms, preferring, apparently, to glare down at her.

CeCe stiffened. Hunter was . . . well, he was special. The

special-est—was that even a word?—boy she'd ever met. And she—

"I love him," she said softly, not thinking what the words would mean to Colin, who couldn't begin to understand her relationship with Hunter.

He was hers, but not.

Kind of like the man sitting next to her had been.

Colin made a noise very much like a growl and scowled at her. "You *love* him?"

It was truly a pleasure to make a man like Colin McGregor squirm. One might be frightened because he was huge, with arms like tree trunks, shoulders nearly twice the breadth of hers, brows dark black and yanked together, but Colin had never hurt her.

Not physically anyway.

And besides that, he couldn't possibly begin to understand what her relationship with Hunter was.

She'd been part nanny, part mother, part sister, and *all* friend to the sick little boy before he'd gotten a heart transplant the previous year. Now, he was still a friend and a little brother and a son and . . . not hers. He belonged with Abby and Jordan. He had a family. He was happy and adjusted and finally, *finally* healthy.

But he would always hold a chunk of her heart.

"He's eight," she murmured. "Or rather, he's nearly nine now."

Colin stiffened. His eyes were wide, almost panicked, and it only took her a heartbeat to understand why.

"Your math's off," she said lightly. Because she understood with crystal clarity why he was so concerned. "If you'd knocked me up, we'd have a *seven*-year-old."

They'd slept together eight years ago. For the first time. She internally sighed since it had also been the last time. But the crazed look in Colin's eyes wasn't so much because of Hunter or her tattoo or even whether or not she'd been pleased by the events (and yes, she had been, despite fumbling on both their parts). Instead, the terror was because he was worried she might have kept a child from him.

Rage filled her. Did he honestly think she wouldn't have told him when they'd nearly gotten *married*? What would she have done after the wedding? Surprise! Here's the two-year-old you helped create!

Fucking moron.

"Hunter isn't mine," she snapped. "Or yours, either." One earbud in. "He was just a boy I nannied for." She shoved in the other. "And while your family may lie about information that could make or break another person, *I* would never do such a thing. You didn't get me pregnant, Colin, and I thank God every day for that fact."

"What?" His brows rose. "That's not—"

But she didn't hear the rest of his words because she cranked up her audiobook.

And heard all of one sentence before Colin plucked the buds from her ears and snatched her phone from her grip. He glanced down at the screen. "This rubbish comes in audiobooks now?"

Once the brogue would have sent warmth down her spine. Today, that warmth was still present, though it was in the form of embarrassment.

Because the audiobook was about a Scot and an English-woman, the former stealing the latter away and teaching her all there was to know about pleasure and life in the Highlands. It was filled with kilts and beards, with sporrans and fabulous dresses and it was . . . so fucking embarrassing.

Once, he'd been *her* Highlander.

She'd drooled over his kilt, admired his legs as he'd straddled his mount.

He'd shown her pleasure. A single night of glorious, soul-shattering pleasure before disappearing from her life for years.

"Give that back," she hissed, but he merely ignored her and put one of the earbuds in and—horror of all freaking horrors—began to listen in.

A strand of black hair curled across his forehead as he turned his stare to hers.

His innocent stare. Except it wasn't innocent. The man next to her was about as far from that sentiment as one could humanly be.

"Stop," she snapped, extending her hand. "You're not cute, and the guileless little boy eyes won't work on me. Give. Me. My. Phone."

"I don't sound like that," he muttered, but took out the earbud and returned her cell. "That is the most inaccurate genre of books I've ever come across. I can't believe you still read—"

"I don't care if it's accurate or not"—she glowered—"but these authors do a ton of research, so I have faith in them. And plus, it's *fiction*. I'm allowed to get lost in the story, just for the pleasure of it. Just because I enjoy it." She stopped, chest heaving, cheeks hot. She hated when people judged her because of the books she read. So, what if she read romance? The stories and writing were good, and didn't everyone deserve a happily-ever-after?

Even if those HEAs didn't always materialize in real life.

"If you want to really learn about Scotland, you should read a history book," he said. "Or maybe a biography. Or *visit*."

Her heart squeezed tight at the old argument they'd had on a regular basis. "I've read loads of history books," she whispered. "And I did visit. Or don't you remember?"

Blue eyes held hers. "I remember." A pause. "All too well."

Ouch.

She blinked before glancing down at her hands. "Yeah, well. I wasn't exactly planning on this."

"On what?" He turned to face her more fully, his elbow encroaching on her armrest, his scent teasing her nose, that damned lock of hair still falling across his forehead and making her ache to smooth it back into place. "On being trapped next to me for twelve hours?"

She shook her head. "On ever seeing you again."

FIVE

Colin

THE WORDS WERE a physical blow to Colin's gut. He knew CeCe was hurt. That *he'd* hurt her. But frankly, they'd hurt each other, and to actually hear her speak words like that aloud was brutal.

On what?

On ever seeing you again.

Like an idiot, he'd pressed her, and like a moron, he'd expected to hear something different. Some explanation for why she'd left him for his best friend. Why the woman he'd imagined spending the rest of his life with had betrayed him so deeply and abandoned him.

"Well, you nearly accomplished it," he said. "Do you live in San Francisco now? Or was that just a stopover?"

She sighed. "Are we really doing this?"

"Doing what?"

"Small talk." Her words were like ice, little frosty bullets that threatened to wound. "Pretending to be old friends."

His hold on his temper was getting decidedly more tenuous.

He bent so his nose was nearly pressed to hers. "You left, sweet-heart. *You left me.* So, if anyone has a right to be pissed, it's me. I needed you, and you fucking *left.*"

Her shoulders had risen with each of his snapped state-ments until they were practically covering her ears. He'd hated when she used to do that, curling into herself, protecting rather than fighting.

She'd done that, he remembered, far too often with his family during their engagement, after he'd won her back the first time. When his family had lobbed their quote, unquote *friendly* rejoinders her way.

And she'd done it that day on the cliffside eight years before when she'd declared her love for him and he'd panicked, before walking away from her.

But now CeCe dropped her shoulders, and *her* temper joined the party. "I left? *I. Left? You—*" Her eyes closed for a heartbeat, and he watched a deep breath slide through her lungs. "You know what? It doesn't matter."

It mattered to him. A whole hell of a lot.

But she was still talking, and he soaked up all the informa-tion he could.

"I live north of the city. I've"—she shook her head—"I was at loose ends for a while, but then I got the job as a nanny. Hunter is the sweetest boy."

Her lips curved, teasing him, reminding him of how it had been to kiss that smile, to twine his hand through her hair, tug her close, and feel those lips against his.

"He got sick pretty young and needed a heart transplant. But he got one last year and—"

Colin touched her hand when she faltered, and those green eyes went shiny with tears.

"He's just so much better now. Healthy and running and . . . I just love him so much." She sniffed. "But he doesn't need me anymore, and so I'm"—she laughed darkly—"God, I don't even know why I'm telling you any of this."

"Except that maybe I understand what it's like to be at a crossroads."

CeCe froze and glanced up at him. After a moment, she murmured, "Yeah. I suppose you would."

"How are your parents?"

It was the wrong question. Her face closed down, and she slipped her hand out from beneath his, clutching it to her chest as though he'd burned her.

And maybe he had.

"They're fine."

"Cecilia." He reached for her again, cursing under his breath when she cringed away from him. "What happened?"

"You know what happened," she said, her words soft and yet somehow more piercing than her harsh tone from earlier. "They said if I went, they were done." A shrug. "And I went."

"*What?*" He'd expected them to have come to their senses, to have put aside the grudge they'd harbored when she'd chosen not to go to their preferred college.

How could they have shut her out?

An unpleasant feeling unfurled in his stomach. Same way he had, he supposed.

She laughed, but it sounded off. "Oh, Colin." The pity was palpable. "I know you're used to breaking your promises, but there are plenty of people who hold firm to theirs." Another laugh, this one filled with so much fatigue that it physically made his heart ache. "And my parents have always been nothing but firm."

His tongue was glued to the roof of his mouth. She implied that he'd broken *his* promises? She was the one who'd betrayed him and then left. But more than that, how could her parents have abandoned her? How could they have just left her to make her own way because she hadn't done exactly as they wished?

What the fuck was wrong with them?

He hadn't realized that he'd spoken the last aloud until CeCe touched his hand. "I knew what I was getting into. And I was a grown woman. It was time that I found my own way."

"You were *twenty*."

She pulled her hand back, twisting in her seat so that she faced him, but also so she was physically as far as possible from him. "An adult."

He scoffed. "A foolish one." Everyone was an idiot at twenty.

Hurt flashed across her emerald eyes, but she nodded before saying softly, "Yes. Yes, I was."

The foolish for trusting *him* was only implied, but it still weighted the air between them.

"Why did you leave me? Why did you run off with Ewan?" He finally asked it outright, needing to hear it from her lips. Maybe then—

Maybe *what*?

"You really don't remember?" she asked.

He shook his head. "I remember the whiskey. I remember seeing the papers, the journal, the *pictures*. But the rest of it is black." He thrust a hand through his hair. "When I woke up, you were gone. And I couldn't find you."

"Colin." She sighed. "I can't do this. Not again."

Another clench of his gut. "But—"

She waved a hand through the air in a slicing motion. "I *had* to go. Can't we just leave it at that?"

No. They damn well couldn't. Not when he'd pictured her in his arms for eternity. Not when he'd imagined their children. Not when he'd fantasized about waking every morning next to her. Not when—

"And it was for the best anyway. We were too young, too immature. It would have never worked out."

"*It would have worked out.*" He pressed his thumb to her lips when she opened her mouth to protest. "I would have bloody well fought tooth and nail to make it work."

Her eyes filled with tears again, making those green irises shine with a force that hit him exactly where it hurt.

"Except you didn't fight for me, Colin." She yanked her head back. "*You didn't.*"

SIX

Colin

HE STARED into CeCe's eyes, hating that they were filled with unshed tears. That *he* had been the cause of her hurt.

"Except you didn't fight for me, Colin," she'd said.

He hadn't gotten a chance to respond because Cecilia jumped out of her seat and bolted for the bathroom. By the time she came out, ten minutes later, the flight attendants were serving breakfast and she had plenty of time to erect her walls of privacy against him.

Namely those earbuds.

But also, by striking up a conversation with the woman in front of them, who'd dropped a book that CeCe had returned.

By the time the women had finished chatting and the breakfast plates were cleared, the plane was descending.

And Colin was trapped beside her, unable to break the silence.

Well, *unable* wasn't the correct word.

He *could* just start talking. The trouble was he didn't even know where to begin. The past was a series of landmines between them, and he'd always thought that he was the one most wronged, that CeCe had returned to Scotland the second time to punish him for his idiotic immaturity of their first summer together, that she'd seduced him and purposely broken his heart because he'd hurt her in the past. Now, he was wondering if it were possible that he'd gotten it all wrong.

His mother, *hell*, even his sister had confirmed that Cecilia had run off with his best friend—*former* best friend, that was.

But she'd said he hadn't fought for her.

Was it possible . . . could he have it all wrong?

Especially because Colin was beginning to understand that his family could sometimes manipulate him.

It was both fortunate and not, that he'd witnessed the manipulation firsthand when they had sabotaged his buyout of Jordan O'Keith's technology firm the previous year. They'd cost him millions of dollars and hundreds of hours of his and his employees' time because they *"couldn't stomach being associated with an American."*

It was only by pure dumb luck that he'd run into Heather O'Keith, Jordan's half-sister and the woman who'd ended up buying out InDTech, now named RoboTech, at a conference a few months ago and had been able to explain himself.

He'd apologized, knowing there was no going back and that the millions were lost for eternity.

But Heather had surprised him by offering to hear his ideas for a mutually beneficial working relationship . . . if he had any. Which he hadn't, of course. Not at that time, anyway. He'd been stuck on the missed opportunity and disappointed he wasn't working with technology that would truly make the world a better place.

So, he'd told her he would put something together and contact her with an agreement she couldn't refuse.

What a fanciful thought. She'd rebuffed his first three offers, until finally he'd struck the right cord, and they'd begun brainstorming on unmanned aircraft technology and how it could be implemented in the third world.

War zones. Natural disasters. How could they get food, water, and medical supplies in when the conditions were too dangerous for personnel?

They didn't have all the answers yet, but now his biomedical robotic company was going to be working closely with RoboTech for the next five years on developing such technology.

He was finally getting close to something that wasn't just money, that wasn't solely based on shareholders and profit-and-loss statements.

Colin was finally doing something worthwhile.

It had taken him long enough.

Still, Heather's initial refusals on his projects had changed him in a way he hadn't expected. Typically, if someone didn't want to work with him, he said fuck off and went and completed the project on his own. And when it was complete, he then made it his life's duty to make them regret the rejection.

So, there were not many people who didn't work with him.

Until Heather.

"You going to go cry to mama?" she'd interrupted as they'd spoken over the phone, scorn in her every syllable when he'd begun to threaten along his usual tack. *"Not used to being subpar? Going to run off and pout like a little boy who doesn't want to try harder to make it better?"*

He'd been so infuriated that his words had stoppered up in his throat.

"RoboTech is the best," she'd gone on. *"And we never stop trying to get better. Until you're ready to be all in with that, I'm sorry, but both you and your projects are useless to me."*

And then she'd hung up.

He'd sat there, stunned, surprised, infuriated. But she'd been right.

He *had* been a spoiled brat in his business dealings, throwing his temper around when he didn't get his way.

He'd been a twenty-eight-year-old man throwing a bloody tantrum.

Pathetic.

Colin was more thankful for Heather than she would ever know. She'd propelled him into a change for the better, and he was finally, *finally* a man who could hold his head high.

Pride was a fickle beast, and he'd always gripped his tightly —whether he'd been right or wrong or somewhere in between. But Heather had helped him see differently, and so he was truly on a healthier path now.

His businesses functioned better, he wasn't chained to a desk all day, every day, and he was finally finding a way out of the dark tunnel that had been his life after his father's death.

And what was the first thing he'd seen after emerging from the opposite end?

Cecilia.

More beautiful than ever, but with shadows in her eyes and hurt coloring every word.

What had he done to her?

What had his family done?

They'd witnessed her running off with Ewan Campbell. He'd *seen* the proof in pictures.

But what if he'd been wrong?

What if he'd stopped searching for Cecilia too soon? What if—?

Fuck.

He was filled to the brim with "what ifs" and not any of them made a difference. Because she was here. Now. And this time, he wasn't going to let her go.

SEVEN

Cecilia

CECILIA WAS thankful to be staying in London for a night. She wouldn't really get to see anything, but she planned on a longer stopover on her way back to the States.

For now, she was happy for a hotel, some non-airplane food, along with a hot shower and soft bed.

Not that she'd been uncomfortable in Colin's arms.

"Shut up," she muttered, reaching for her phone and stuffing it into her tote bag, along with her pillow, her lip balm, and the seventy-three other things she'd managed to strew around during the twelve-hour flight.

"Pardon?" Colin's voice was slightly rasped, almost sounding unused, and not at all indicative of the fact that they'd just been arguing an hour before.

"Sorry," she said. "I was talking to myself."

His lips twitched, his beard glinting slightly in the airplane's overhead lights. And why hadn't she noticed it earlier?

The beard was very Chris Evans as Captain America—the second Avengers version where he looked all yummy and scruffy and beyond sexy. Except Colin was a Scot and his accent added a whole other layer of deliciousness that was truly unfair to the female populace.

"So. Not. Fair."

One black brow sprang up.

She sighed, mentally slapping herself. "Sorry. I'm doing it again."

He grinned and her panties melted, just slipped right down off her thighs. Okay fine, so the underwear magic act was a complete and utter fantasy, but his effect on her lady parts was not.

She still wanted him.

Once had definitely not been enough, and their single attempt at learning one another certainly highlighted that fact.

He'd given her an orgasm . . . before penetration, that was, but he'd promised her more, better, *longer* later.

Only later had never come. Not even during their short-term engagement—his family had made sure of that.

It had taken years of self-exploration and several diligent partners for her to understand her own body. For sex to finally be spectacular. Or, if maybe not spectacular, then at least pretty damned good.

"I always liked it when you did that."

For a moment, she panicked, thinking she'd been expounding upon her sexual delights aloud before she realized that Colin was referring to her proclivity for talking to herself.

"Well." She shrugged. "Apparently, it's a habit I won't ever be able to shake."

Blue eyes locked with hers. "I hope you don't ever change."

She gave him a sad smile. "Everyone changes, Colin. It's a fact of life."

"I was hoping you'd say that because—"

"Ladies and gentlemen, please ensure your tray tables and

seatbacks . . ." came the flight attendant's voice through the loudspeakers, declaring them ready for landing before discussing connections and the weather in London.

Cecilia deliberately focused on the woman's words as she opened her window shade and stared out at the landscape.

But she wasn't really taking in the view of the gorgeous green countryside or the massive sprawl that was London. Instead, she was trying to forget Colin's words.

"I was hoping you'd say that because—"

Because what?

No. It didn't matter. The rest of that sentence was *not* important.

Except it was.

She closed her eyes.

Dammit.

The rest of that sentence was really, *really* important.

HER BAGS WERE LOST.

She was planning a trip to Finland with no end date, followed by backpacking around Europe, also with no deadline, and her bags were nowhere in sight.

"All right?"

Colin. Of course.

He held his carry-on in one hand and looked dashing and unruffled despite the long flight.

She'd expected him to be long gone after the hellish line she'd had to wait in to get through the passport check while he'd breezed through the other shorter queue.

Stupid sexy Scot.

She turned back to the conveyor belt, but her bag had not miraculously appeared.

And so, her trip was continuing its fabulous start.

"I'm good." CeCe straightened her shoulders and pasted on a smile. "Lovely to chat with you." She turned away but didn't get far. Colin slipped his fingers through the strap on her bag and halted her escape.

"Is this all you brought with you?"

"I'm fine." She lifted her chin in the direction of the airline's well-lit office. "I've had airlines lose my bags before. It's not a huge deal. It'll turn up, so if you'll excuse me . . ."

He released her and she left, not looking back, not daring to make eye contact with him again, lest he see the longing in her eyes.

This was her trip to find herself again, to prove that she was as strong and capable as she hoped to be.

So off she went to file a lost luggage claim.

Like a calm, responsible adult. Not like a mid-twenty-something who wanted to throw a temper tantrum or lie down and cry . . . or better yet, to lie down and *sleep*.

Instead, she adulted.

And hated every minute of it.

EIGHT

Cecilia

CECE FOLDED the printout from the luggage report and smiled at the woman's assurances that her bag would be found and delivered to her hotel by the morning. With an inner sigh, she turned and walked through customs with only her carry-on.

Thank God she'd brought a toothbrush and a change of clothes in her tote.

She checked the signs and started walking in the direction of the taxi stand, the mental image of her forthcoming soft and fluffy mattress almost too much to bear.

"Cecilia." A hand grasped her arm.

"Shit!" She jumped, lost her grip on her bag, and watched as the contents of her long-ass-plane-ride survival kit rolled in all directions.

Her Chapstick skidded end over end until it slid under a fully occupied row of chairs, her phone skittered beneath a massive rolling suitcase guided haphazardly by a small child and narrowly missed being crushed by its menacing metal wheels. Her pencils and sketchpad scattered in all directions and her clothes . . . no, her underwear, *that* went floating across the floor, wafting to a gentle stop on Colin's foot.

He bent and picked up the flimsy scrap of deep green lace— it matched her eyes, okay? And plus, a girl needed to feel sexy every once in a while.

Or at least that was what Bec had said when she'd gifted Cecilia a trunkful of expensive lingerie before her trip.

"For those sexy European guys," she'd mock-whispered before her face had gone deadly serious in that fierce lawyer mask of hers. *"And for you. Because you're amazing and beautiful and deserve to feel that way."*

Colin coughed, cheeks going faintly pink. "I-uh . . . sorry about that. I didn't mean to startle you." He held the ridiculously small thong clenched in his fist, and the sight made her stomach tighten.

Well, not just her *stomach*. She got that squidgy feeling just beneath her belly button, traveling lower, throbbing, aching, until her thighs squeezed together in a vain attempt at soothing that empty feeling within her.

She blinked before regaining her senses.

Her heart was empty, and she was going to Finland to fill it with beautiful green-tinted lights and the wide-open night sky. There would be snow and animals and a glass-roofed cabin of her own. She was going to sort out the loneliness inside her, finally find her place in the world.

And that place didn't include Colin or his yummy hands *or* her panties scrunched up all sexily in his palms.

Enough.

In a quick movement, she snatched her underwear from Colin's hand and stuffed it into her bag. Then she began crouch-walking as she hurried to gather up all her other items.

Which didn't take long because he helped.

Colin McGregor just could not take a hint.

"Cecilia—" he began but coughed again, probably because she'd just stuffed an entire string of condoms back into her tote.

Protection wasn't just a woman's responsibility, but damned if she was going to rely on a man to keep her safe.

That's what led to accidental pregnancies, and *that* wasn't a romance novel trope she was interested in living . . . not in real life anyway. Between the pages of a book was another thing entirely.

"Goodbye, Colin," she murmured, slinging her bag onto her shoulder.

"Wait." He hesitated before touching her arm again. "Let me see you safely to your hotel." When she started to shake her head, he gave her puppy dog eyes. And the infuriating man gave damned good puppy dog eyes. "Please, CeCe. I know I don't deserve your consideration, but will you at least let me know that you're safe and sound?"

She sighed. Was she seriously considering spending more time in a confined space with the man who'd broken her heart twice?

Ugh. She totally was.

"Fine," she said, giving in because she was too tired to fight, too tired to resist stealing just a little bit more of Colin.

He smiled, and the brilliance of it sucked the air from her lungs. *God*, he had the best freaking smile, wide and slightly crooked on one end, his teeth straight and white but not perfectly aligned. That little bit of imperfection mixed into all of the flawlessness that was Colin McGregor just added a whole other layer.

It was too much, and it wasn't enough.

She wanted him. She was scared.

She was hurt but remembered the great times they'd had together. The brilliant moments when they were alone, when she was with someone who saw her as her true self.

When she'd belonged.

Sadness swept through her, and she dropped her eyes to the floor, hurting, absolutely *aching* for the loss of that time in her life, no matter how brief it had been.

"Cecilia?"

She forced her gaze up, made her lips tip into a smile. "Should we go?"

"Sweetheart?" A brush of his thumb across her cheek. "What is it?"

Her heart turned over in her chest, that long old scar throbbing. But she couldn't tell Colin that. Not now, not here, not after all this time. "I'm tired," she said. "Can we go?"

Blue eyes searched hers for a long moment before he nodded. "Of course."

He grabbed her bag, slinging it over his arm, and pointed in the direction of the automatic doors.

Cecilia frowned. "Where's *your* bag?"

"The driver has it." He nodded at the man wearing a black suit and tie with a pristine white button down, standing next to a black sedan. "Thanks for waiting, Danny."

Danny nodded, opening the door without a word, but the look he gave her was assessing.

And immediately made her spine go stiff.

She'd seen that look before. Too many times over. From his family. From his friends. She was the calculating American trying to take advantage.

"You know—" She hesitated, ready to say, 'fuck it all' and take a cab like her original plan, but Colin had anticipated her actions. He snagged her wrist and tugged her into the car in a move so quick the rest of her sentence was swallowed up in a gasp and the sound of the door closing.

"Hotel." He gripped her chin between his thumb and forefinger. "Then I'll leave you to your life."

Her breath caught. In relief? In disappointment?

Who knew?

Except . . . she *knew*.

And what she knew but didn't want to admit, even to herself, was that those words left her with a trace of displeasure —no, *more* than a trace. What she felt was a torrent of regret that was nearly impossible to ignore. She should have fought, should have done something.

But she'd been young and vulnerable and . . . *so damned hurt*.

So, she ignored the blip of sorrow at the thought of never seeing Colin again.

She tucked that hurt down, shoved it all away, and did what she did best.

Pretended to be completely fine despite the fact that she was totally shattered inside.

———

LONDON WAS BEAUTIFUL. The buildings were like nothing she'd seen before. Tall, huge walls of gorgeous architecture full to the brim with arches and curls and wooden doors. Brick houses transformed into gothic churches before pivoting again into another style and then another as traffic weaved and bobbed and turned through narrow and twisted streets.

Every building was multistoried and towered over the car. Which should have made her feel closed in.

But instead she felt safe and cozy, like she was tucked snugly under a soft comforter.

London was nothing like her little town north of San Francisco.

There were multistory buildings at home, of course, but not

like this. Not packed in, crowded together, taking up every millimeter of available space.

Good thing she wasn't claustrophobic.

"Different from Scotland, isn't it?"

Cecilia stiffened, somehow having forgotten that she was trapped in a car with Colin. She removed her hand from where it was pressed against the window, purposefully wiped what was almost certainly a sappy smile from her face, and turned to face him.

They were nearing the clogged streets close to Buckingham Palace, and she knew her hotel wouldn't be far off.

Though . . . traffic.

They could be trapped for days.

Le. Sigh.

It was easier to be closed off from Colin when he was more of a painful memory rather than a living, breathing human.

Who was nice and waited for her and gave her rides and—

Broke your heart, girlfriend, she imagined Seraphina saying. Her beautiful blonde bombshell of a friend would tell her to woman up and harden her heart. *Forget him. Move on and hook up with a hot Finnish guy. They make man buns look sexy.*

She just wished it were that easy.

Because amongst the painful memories were good ones. More than the bad, more than the ones that shattered her teenage fantasies.

She sighed. This trip was supposed to be about relaxing, enjoying herself after spending so long wrapped up in Hunter's appointments and treatments and medications. This was supposed to be about her having an adventure where she wasn't trying to think of ways to get Carter—Abby and Jordan's baby— to eat peas when the little toddler hated all foods that were green.

This—

She sighed again, wanting to slap herself. She shouldn't be missing them. It hadn't even been a day.

Fingers on her cheek startled her.

"You okay?" Colin asked.

She leaned into his touch, inhaling the spicy scent that was solely Colin—leather and sandalwood and pine.

"I—"

Then she realized who she was leaning closer toward, whose hand was cradling her face, and who apparently had as big a hold on her body and mind as ever.

P.A.T.H.E.T.I.C.

That was her.

"London is different than Scotland," she said, finally getting a grip and circling back to safer topics than her idiotic brain and heart. "I mean, all I'd seen of it before was Heathrow, and that wasn't exciting. And I know it doesn't make sense for my travel plans, with me leaving for Finland tomorrow, but I couldn't miss a chance to be here without at least seeing Buckingham Palace and Hyde Park—"

"You're leaving *tomorrow*?"

The car slowed, pulling to a stop at the curb. And *seriously*, she was tipping this driver big time.

CeCe took one glance at Colin's stormy expression—the one that used to make her crazy. Crazy to kiss him and smooth it out. Crazy to piss him off further so he'd yank her close and kiss *her* with all that pent-up frustration. Crazy to—

Run.

"Oh look, we're here," she said, popping the door handle and climbing out onto the sidewalk, thankful that they were on the "wrong" side of the road, so she didn't have to clamber over Colin's legs.

Because it wouldn't be clambering over so much as clambering *onto,* and that would be very dangerous indeed.

She grabbed her tote bag, tucking it over her shoulder while slamming the door shut, and thrust a fifty-pound note at the surprised driver, who was just sliding out of the car.

She needed to get to her room, slam the deadbolt, and hide.

The smiling attendant waved her forward, and CeCe handed over her passport all while trying not to glance behind her like she was a fugitive on the run.

This just in . . . she felt like one.

"Here you go," the woman said. "You've got a lovely room on the fifth floor. You'll find the elevator right down that hall."

Cecilia thanked her, hurrying away from the desk and ignoring the fact that the space between her shoulder blades was prickling.

Risking a quick glance back gained her nothing. Colin was nowhere in sight. He'd left after she'd so unceremoniously slammed the car door in his face.

Obviously.

So, what if she felt the tiniest bit disappointed and, well, guilty for slamming said door in said handsome, dark, and brooding face?

She pressed the button for the elevator, stood back when the doors dinged open, and then started to select the fifth floor.

The hairs on her nape rose before he even spoke.

As though she had a built-in Colin-detector.

And frankly, she needed to face facts. She did have a built-in Colin-detector.

It was called her vagina.

As in, it got wet every time he was nearby.

"You actually need to press six," he murmured from too close behind her, reaching over her shoulder to push the button with that number. "Floors are counted differently in England than the United States. Here, they have a ground floor and *then* the numbers start counting up from one."

CeCe glanced down at the envelope housing her room key and sure enough, she was in room six-twenty-two.

Fifth floor. Lies.

Shaking her head as the doors slid closed, she stuck her room key in her pocket and then sighed, dropping her chin to her chest, warring with herself—

"Fuck it," she muttered, sliding her tote bag from her shoulder and letting it fall with a *thump* to the floor. She whipped around, launched herself at Colin.

He jumped and fumbled, and she thought for sure they were both going down, but then he regrouped, regaining his balance and holding her tight against his chest.

And—*God*—it felt fantastic, being in his arms, being this close.

"Cecilia?" he asked, blue eyes wide but filling rapidly with heat.

He felt it, too. He understood the attraction, the never-ending pull that seemed to yank them together time and time again.

That attraction was the only reason—the *only* reason, take that her damned smug conscience—that she kissed him.

And promptly lost her head.

NINE

Colin

COLIN SPENT APPROXIMATELY six seconds in heaven before it was torn from his arms.

Or rather, before CeCe ripped *herself* from his hold.

He'd had just a tease of soft curves and floral scents, felt the press of her lips, her breasts, her tongue against him.

Then the bloody elevator had dinged, its doors had slid open, and she'd run.

Again.

This pattern was getting frustrating.

He slammed his fist against the metal panel as it tried to slide closed and bent to pick up the paper envelope that had fallen from Cecilia's pocket when she'd thrown herself into his arms. She'd grabbed her tote bag, so there was that, but she wouldn't be getting far without a room key.

Sighing, he tucked his messenger bag over one shoulder and left the elevator, bracing himself for her presence, for the punch to the gut that stole his breath every time he saw her.

She was beautiful, inside and out, there was no doubt about that. But she was also . . . scared. Hurting.

And he wanted the full story, for fuck's sake.

Not a piece of information here and there. Not a slice of the past and vague words. He wanted to know what had happened six years ago.

Because by all rights, *he* should be the wounded one.

But Colin had the feeling that he wasn't.

He glanced at the key holder in his palm, searched out the sign on the wall, and headed in the direction of Cecilia's room.

She wasn't far, around one corner, head in her hands, bag still over one arm but resting on the floor, as she squatted against a door.

He ignored the jump of his pulse and stretched an arm over her head, swiping the key against the lock. It disengaged with a *click.* When he shoved it open, bright green eyes flew up to his, and her mouth opened, no doubt to put him off again.

A shake of his head, a swift movement to scoop her up off the floor.

"Col—"

"Hush." He growled when she flailed her arms, that damned annoying tote bag whacking him in the head. He slid it free from her arm, then set it carefully on the luggage stand before carrying CeCe further into the room, flipping switches all the way.

"*Colin.*"

He didn't bother to reply. Instead, he ripped the comforter free of the mattress with one hand.

"Hey! You can't—*oof!*"

He took a breath, shaking off the tempting sight of the woman he'd obsessed over for years, hair mussed, looking up from a bed at him in invitation.

No. Confusion. With a little irritation mixed in.

Colin bent and removed her shoes, lining them up next to the nightstand, before turning back and staring at CeCe.

Yes, it was probably creepy.

No, he couldn't stop himself.

Especially when her lips parted and there *was* a hint of invitation in her expression. He leaned down, felt the hot whoosh of her breath on his mouth, and kissed her . . . on the cheek.

"Good night, sweetheart," he murmured, pulling up the blanket and tucking it around her. Gritting his teeth, he set the keycard on the nightstand and rose to his feet.

And then he did the opposite of what every cell in his body was demanding—namely stripping CeCe naked, leaving her limp with orgasms, holding her close afterward, whispering all the words he'd felt, *still* felt, into her ear, and watching her fall asleep.

Did she still snore in soft little puffs of air?

Would she still whisper his name and snuggle closer?

Could they possibly forget the past and find a way to build something new?

He wanted to find out the answers to all those questions. He wanted her body, her heart, her soul.

He wanted *her*.

That was why he had to leave.

Colin tried to ignore the fact that she didn't stop him as he went.

It didn't work.

HOTEL BARS WERE THE WORST. The scourge of the earth, the cesspool of all humanity, the bottom of the proverbial barrel.

Either that or he was being dramatic.

Okay, he *was* being dramatic.

And that wasn't like him.

But he'd sent his driver away, intending to walk the city until his nerves settled. The trouble was he had only made it as far as the hotel bar.

He had always felt like this . . . not about the bar and not acting like a gross creeper stalking a woman who wanted nothing to do with him. Rather, he meant that it had always felt as though there were a piece of string attaching him to Cecilia. It had been stretched taut, threatening to snap for many years, and now that he'd found her, he didn't have the strength to risk that tenuous position once more.

What if he couldn't find her again?

Dramatic meet maudlin meet terrible Shakespeare-esque drama.

He should have just talked to her when he'd been in her room.

Better that than brooding over a bottle of whiskey like a pathetic idiot.

"Another?" the bartender asked when Colin drained the last drops from his glass.

"No, thanks." He shook his head and tossed enough bills on the bar top to cover his tab plus a healthy tip. The man had been quick, efficient, and didn't ask nosy questions.

But Colin was bleary-eyed, exhausted after the flight, and the days had been packed with meetings before then, and he really needed to sleep.

He was also slightly drunk.

Which was probably why he headed to the elevators rather than pulling out his cell and calling his driver. He pressed the button for the fifth floor and waited calmly—albeit with a slightly faltering stance . . . the floor's fault for not being level, thank him very much—as the elevator rose.

Then he pulled out the spare key to CeCe's room, the one

he'd put in his pocket earlier for *safekeeping*, and unlocked the door.

It was mostly dark, with only the bedside lamp on, and she'd fallen asleep with a book on her chest.

One of those bloody historical romances.

For fuck's sake.

He carefully picked it up, lest it stab her in the eye or something as she slept, and started to close it. Only a word caught his eye. Then a sentence.

Then a *scene*.

And hot damn, *what* a scene.

He sank to the floor next to the bed and turned the page.

And another. And another. And . . . he read the whole damned thing. The sex, the horses, the kilts, the conflict that drove the hero and heroine apart—conflict driven by the hero's intervening family that left a nasty aftertaste in his mouth. He even read the happy ending and the epilogue where their castle was full of children and the couple lived in a state of unending bliss.

The book made him sigh like a sappy sod, and it made him ache. To *long* for the fictional happily ever after.

It also made him sleepy, and Colin found himself listing to the side, curling up next to the bed, and closing his eyes.

TEN

Cecilia

CECILIA WOKE with her mouth feeling as though she'd swallowed an entire desert worth of sand. Her breath certainly could have made any desert-dwelling creature drop dead on the spot.

She never went to bed without brushing her teeth, without religiously using mouthwash and flossing, and now she'd done so twice in the last day.

Gross.

But she'd been so exhausted—emotionally and physically— after everything that had happened with Colin, that she hadn't moved from the bed, except to grab a book, toss her leggings to the floor, and slip off her bra.

She'd waited for him to come back, to knock at the door and demand answers.

He hadn't.

And she wasn't disappointed.

Because she was a strong independent woman and was fine on her own. Cue her wagging finger and her podium-worthy rant. She didn't need a man, dammit. She was traveling through Europe. She had plans. She—

Had been frozen in place by his kiss. On her cheek.

Ugh.

Running her tongue over her teeth and wincing at the furry feeling, CeCe tossed the covers back and stood.

Who knew what hour it was, but she'd slept enough of her time away in London already. She wanted to go see Buckingham Palace and the Crown Jewels. And if she had time, she wanted to walk through Hyde Park with a coffee.

Dropping her chin to her chest, she took a moment to stretch out her stiff neck. No matter how expensive the room, hotel pillows still sucked.

A sigh. One more quick stretch, and she headed for the bathroom. Or attempted to, anyway, because she had only taken one step in that direction before she tripped over something.

No. Some*one.*

A huge, male someone.

Her scream caught in her throat, and she sucked in more air, trying to clear it, before she realized the male someone was actually a Scottish male someone named Colin.

"Shit," she hissed, heart pounding, hand coming to her throat.

Colin was sleeping on the floor between the bed and the hotel wall, on the gross, hard industrial carpet. And he had . . . her *book?* It was resting open on his chest, rising and falling with each of his breaths.

He had read it?

Oh, God.

Heat scorched her cheeks. The book was a steamy one, and *of course* the hero was Scottish and had broken the heroine's heart in the past.

Which was too damned close to home, but she hadn't been

able to stop herself from finishing it, from crying at their trials, and then sighing in contentment when they'd finally found their happily-ever-after.

CeCe reached for the book, wanting to get it far away from Colin. Frankly, she wanted to chuck it out the window, but since that was probably sealed shut, she'd settle for it to be shoved deep down into her tote bag, never to been seen by steely blue eyes again.

The book's cover was smooth beneath her fingers, that soft, almost velvet-like feel that some paperbacks had.

The spine was in good shape, hardly creased, but then again, she was very careful with her books in general.

Not the point at the moment, yet a nice distraction, nonetheless.

But the distraction wasn't to last because the moment she caught a whiff of his scent, sandalwood with a hint of whiskey, she was ensnared.

Enraptured.

Entranced.

Her hand slid from the book to Colin's chest, resting lightly as she shifted her position, so her knees were next to his shoulder. And she studied the man, truly looked at him for the first time in years.

Not quick glances before avoiding his gaze, dodging old memories and pain. Not a flick of her eyes then away because he was so beautiful and hot and sexy and . . . overwhelming.

She *really* looked at him.

And noticed the changes in his face, the faint wrinkles around his eyes, the beard covering his cheeks and chin. It was a deep black, but there were a few gray hairs here and there. Enough of the silvery strands that for the first time she stopped to wonder about all that Colin had been through.

She'd been so wrapped up in what happened to *her* that she hadn't stopped to consider him.

Wow. So, that was what guilt felt like.

Snorting at herself, she turned her eyes back to Colin. A curl of hair had slipped over his forehead, and she smoothed it back before starting to stand.

"You're in dangerous territory, sweetheart," came his rumbling, sleep-laden voice, hand snaking out to wrap around her wrist.

"C-Colin," she stammered. "I j-just—"

"You're the most beautiful thing I've ever seen," he said.

Or rather *whiskey-ed*.

Holy entire bottle of the amber concoction, Batman.

"You're drunk," she said.

He shook his head, goofy smile on his face.

"You smell like you took a bath in a distillery," she told him, slipping her wrist free of his grasp.

He tilted his head in the direction of his armpit and wrinkled his nose. His face fell.

That puppy dog expression had always been too much for her. The need to comfort him was compulsory and impossible to resist. "Yours is still my favorite smell in the world," she blurted.

Then wished she'd kept her damned mouth shut because it revealed *way* too much.

The last bit of sleep slipped from Colin's eyes. They sharpened, and she quickly stood.

"I should ask why you're in my room, but I'm not going—" Her breath hitched when his hand went to her ankle, rough fingers tracing gently on the bare skin there. She cleared her throat. "I'm going to take a shower."

"Want company?"

Her heart clenched and her . . . well. Suffice to say that she had a lady boner.

He was fully clothed, touching one of the most innocuous parts of her body, and she had a serious moisture problem.

Which he could probably see, since she was standing almost directly over him.

His fingers slipped higher, tracing little circles along the back of her calf, her knee, teasing at her thigh.

"I-I—"

He leaned up onto one elbow and those fingers slipped higher, until one tip slipped under the elastic of her underwear.

Just the tip.

She giggled.

She couldn't help it. Bec, Abby, and Seraphina had corrupted her.

They were bad influences, especially because they would have encouraged her to . . . well, *encourage* Colin.

And she wanted to. Really, she did. Forget the past in that moment. She had a sexy Scot with his finger in her panties, and she was wound so tight that it wouldn't take more than a brush of said finger to send her toppling.

But he was drunk.

"You're going to say no," he murmured, slipping more of his hand under the elastic and cupping her ass with one rough palm. "I know you are."

She nodded. "I'm going to say no." Then added in a mutter meant for her ears only, "Not that I want to."

Except apparently not quiet enough because Colin's lips curved and his free hand came up, cupping her other cheek. "I can make you feel good," he said, and she knew he could. He *had*.

But. He. Was. Drunk.

"Climb into the bed," she said, pushing his hands down and out of her underwear.

He scrambled up to his feet in a movement way too fast for

someone who was inebriated. His arm slid around her waist and his mouth was on hers before she had a chance to realize what she'd said.

She'd meant for *him* to climb into bed. By himself.

Except she was there. With him. Surrounded by his scent, pressed into the mattress by his bulk. His lips were teasing hers open. His tongue was tangling with hers.

And *fuck* did it feel amazing.

ELEVEN

Colin

CECILIA WAS WRAPPED TIGHTLY against him, pressed firmly against his chest, her legs intertwined with his. Colin moaned and pulled her closer, leaning down to press a kiss to the valley of her breasts.

Then frowned.

Her skin wasn't as soft as he remembered, her curves not as lush. It was almost as though she weren't—

His eyes shot open when something tightened around his neck.

He blinked, searching the space around him, abruptly aware of the cold bed. The linens were soft for a hotel but rough when compared to his woman's skin. And they might have been wound around him, but they were decidedly *unlike* CeCe's curves.

The room was also dark.

Colin cursed and sat up, tearing away the cotton sheet that had somehow become wrapped around his throat.

He saw the clock and cursed, seeing that he'd slept the day away.

And Cecilia was gone.

He knew that in his bones.

"Fuck," he muttered, trying to sift through his sleepy mind, trying to understand how he'd come to wake alone when last he'd remembered, Cecilia had been beneath him on that very bed.

His eyes lit on a note faintly illuminated by the clock and propped onto the bedside table. A little bottle of water and some aspirin were positioned next to it.

Thanks for the lift. Drink the water and take the aspirin. I imagine you'll wake with quite a headache.
Have a nice life,
CeCe
P.S. Don't worry, I paid up the room for another day.
Take care.

COLIN GRUNTED, starting to crumple the note before stopping and instead carefully folding it and putting it into his pocket. "Have a nice life," he muttered, getting out of bed and ignoring the pills. He wasn't a child any longer, and he didn't have a hangover. Yes, he might have drunk a little more than normal the previous night, but he'd been in full possession of his abilities.

Except somehow you fell asleep with the most beautiful woman in the world in your arms, you arsewipe, his brain conveniently reminded him.

Because yes, there was that. He'd had Cecilia in his arms, pliable and warm and delicious and . . .

That was the last thing he remembered.

So, maybe he was slightly out of practice in the whiskey-bingeing department.

Sighing, Colin reached into his satchel and pulled out his phone, checking his emails and sending a text to his assistant to clear his schedule for the foreseeable future.

This was why he'd trained his COO and CFO. So he could have a life.

And he intended to finally have one.

Which was why he called his *other* assistant—the one who specialized in remembering birthdays and selecting the perfect arrangement of flowers for his mother. Joanne had been around the McGregors for decades and had been managing his life since his father died.

She'd also loved Cecilia.

"Joanie," he said. "I have a problem that doesn't involve an artistic arrangement of lilies. Or well, it might involve them. *If* she likes those, which I can't remember—"

"She?" Joanne asked.

He shoved his feet into his shoes, pinning the phone between his ear and shoulder. "I'm getting Cecilia back."

"Finally," Joanne said, and he could almost hear her smile through the airwaves. "But, Colin dear, it's yellow daffodils that she adores. Though, I don't think flowers are going to mend—"

"I don't need flowers," he said. "Though I'm sure I will at some point," he added, filing CeCe's preference in flowers away. "For now, I need you to ready my plane for a flight to Finland."

"Ohhh." Joanne's breath slid out on a sigh. "The northern lights. *Colin*, that was always her dream. It's so romantic."

"Except she left without me."

He heard Joanne's teeth click closed. "Okay, that's less so."

Colin snorted. "I agree." He rattled off the name of the resort he'd seen on the brochure that had fallen out of her bag at the airport. "I need a flight as close as possible to there."

"And a room?"

"No," he said. "I'm hoping she'll take a poor sod in out of the cold."

Joanne huffed. "I wouldn't be so sure, my dear. After what you and your family did to that poor girl—"

Colin's gut tightened. "What Joanie? What did we do?"

A pause. "You don't know?"

His blood iced over. "What?" he asked, barely able to force the word out.

"Colin," she whispered. "Honey, it's—" A sigh. "You were too drunk to remember?"

"I was drunk for weeks," he reminded her.

She sighed again, and the silence stretched between them. "The plane will be ready in two hours."

"Joanie, I need you to tell—"

"No. You and CeCe need to talk this out." A pause. "But, Colin, if you don't want your arse to be frozen solid in Finland, I would be prepared to get on your knees and beg."

Fuck.

"It's that bad?" he asked.

"My boy," she began before clearing her throat. "It's not good."

He opened his mouth to press for details before clamping it closed. The person he needed to discuss this with was Cecilia.

The person he apparently needed to beg for forgiveness was Cecilia.

Colin grabbed his bag and hoped there wouldn't be any snow on the ground because his damn slacks weren't the least bit waterproof.

TWELVE

Cecilia

SHE WAS SITTING on a bench in Hyde Park.

She'd left Colin sleeping in her hotel room much earlier that day, stored her suitcase at the drop-off facility near the hotel, and was now counting the time until she had to leave for the airport.

Buckingham Palace hadn't materialized, but she had gotten a glimpse of the Crown Jewels, and now she was drinking her coffee in the late afternoon sunshine. CeCe had done plenty of traveling on her own, was quite comfortable with silences and navigating cities by herself.

She was happy with that.

Except . . . she wasn't.

Sitting there with a hot carafe of coffee in her hands, the steaming liquid not yet cool enough to drink, CeCe felt very much alone.

"You're over this," she murmured, deliberately turning her focus to a narrow, winding path that veered off to the side. "You've always been alone. You *have* to be over this."

But . . . she wasn't.

She'd always been able to feel self-contained, to be satisfied in that, because she'd spent so much of her time alone. But she hadn't been alone these last few years. She'd had Hunter and Jordan, and now she had Heather and Sera and Abby and Carter along with them.

She had more of a family now than she'd had growing up.

But there was still something empty inside her. Longing. She wanted someone who could be hers, first and foremost. She wanted to be the most important person in someone's life.

Maybe that was selfish, to want to be someone's top priority.

Maybe she needed to understand that love wasn't finite, that just because she wasn't in a relationship, didn't have romantic love that she meant as much to Abby and Jordan and—

No.

That wasn't right either.

Love wasn't finite, but romantic love and friendship weren't the same.

Jordan and Abby had something more.

A more that she was desperate to have, and maybe that made her weak, but also . . . fuck that. For as much as she had been hurt over the years, her ability to care for, to love those around her hadn't been broken. She cared and loved deeply.

So, she fucking deserved to have someone love her in that same way.

Devotedly. Passionately.

She deserved to have a man look at her with the same warmth and affection she saw in Jordan's eyes when he looked at Abby.

"I deserve someone to love every part of me."

Because she knew that she'd loved every part of Colin when they'd been together, the good and bad, the annoying and sweet.

She'd made the mistake of thinking he'd felt the same, and . . . maybe he hadn't.

But also—she thought of the confused expression on the plane, how good his family had been at gaslighting her.

Should she have stayed?

Back then? Should she have ignored the hurtful words, volleyed back some of her own? Should she have fought to understand why he hadn't come to the church?

Now, she would have.

Now, she wouldn't have just stopped at a phone call, or let someone whisk her away to safety.

Now, she'd built a life for herself. Now, she'd taken care of a really sick kid who had gotten through to the other side, who had made her understand that even when things are really fucking hard, they were still worth fighting for.

She pulled her phone out of her pocket and checked the time.

Hours yet.

She stood, her fingers slipping into her other pocket, the one with the keycard in it. The keycard to the room where she'd left Colin sleeping. Maybe seeing him on the plane was a sign that unless she figured out where they went wrong, she would never be able to fully move forward.

But could she go back? What if she was wrong and his family hadn't orchestrated their breakup? What if it was . . . just her?

Sighing, she pocketed her phone, sat back down on the bench, and drank her coffee.

It had cooled too much, didn't taste as good as she had imagined.

Or maybe—she shot to her feet.

Fuck it. She didn't take this trip to be a coward. She was done running from her life, from experiences she wanted to have. She wanted to confront Colin, to tell him what a fucking asshole he'd been, and if that was the only resolution she garnered from the conversation then great, moving on.

But if she got more . . .

Because maybe she'd find something more.

Maybe she'd find a way to fill in that great yawning hole in her heart. By herself. Because *she'd* taken action and decided her future.

To take a risk. Or maybe to play it safe.

But CeCe decided.

Heart thudding, she dumped her coffee in the trash can and made her way through the streets to the Underground, took a train back to the stop for the hotel, and slipped into the elevator.

She almost lost her courage at the door.

But then she lifted her chin, whispered, "You deserve answers." And that gave her the courage to unlock the room, to step inside.

The air was hot and damp, as though someone had just been in the shower.

But the room itself was empty.

Sandalwood and leather and spice . . . and empty.

Disappointment slid through her at being denied her opportunity for resolution, but there was also some pride mixed in. Because she'd been brave enough to not run. Because she'd begun to understand the tangle of feelings inside her. Because she was no longer hiding like a weak ninny.

CeCe had found her strength.

And she wasn't giving it up.

BUMP.

With a sharp gasp, her cell slipped from her fingers and hit the floor of the shuttle van. CeCe winced and watched it slide under the seat in front of her. She'd been trying to return a text from Hunter, had been craning her neck and holding the phone out in a vain attempt to not lose the signal and—

Bump.

The roads weren't ideal.

Bump-bump.

Her cell slid farther forward and very much out of reach.

"Fuck," she muttered and then immediately winced and smiled apologetically when a mom with her two young sons slid her a look.

One of them was about Hunter's age and whispered, or rather attempted to whisper because somehow when kids that age tried to whisper, their voices ended up carrying. And the shuttle they were in wasn't large.

Which meant she heard the little boy's excited statement with crystal clarity. "Mom, she said the *f*-word!"

The younger of the two boys said, "I thought the f-word was fart. She said fu—"

"Oh look," CeCe said, leaning over him to point out the window. "That tree is huge!"

It wasn't really, but it got the boys' attention off one another and their focus out the window rather than on her unfortunate use of the non-fart f-word.

The mom gave her squinty eyes for a second before grinning. "Definitely not the first time they've heard it, nor will it be the last." She shrugged and retrieved CeCe's cell, handing it back to her. "Just trying to keep that one"—she tilted her head in the direction of the littler brother—"out of the loop for as long as possible. He always saves that kind of stuff for the most inopportune moments."

The dad chuckled and slung an arm around his wife's shoulders. "Like the grocery store checkout line."

"And the dentist." The mom grimaced. "*And* the school play."

"I'm sorry," CeCe said again. "I should know better. I'm a nanny."

"*Oh*," the mom said, a faintly calculating note in her voice. "Well then, maybe in payment for your *huge* transgression, we can hit you up for a kid-free night while we're here. How long are you staying?"

"Lizzie," the husband warned. "You're laying it on really thick. You're the one who taught Tate his first bad word, after all."

She wrinkled her nose. "Well, at least he used it correctly."

"At the dentist. 'Get the goddammed thing out of my mouth,' were his exact words if, I remember correctly."

CeCe giggled as the woman popped him on the arm. "Shh! I just got him to stop saying it." She glanced up and smiled. "I'm just kidding about the babysitting," she said as the shuttle slowed to turn into the resort. "But if you're ever lonely and want a little company, here's my cell." She passed over a card. "We'll be here for ten days."

Cecilia glanced down at the paper and noted the California address for a company she didn't recognize. She'd known they were from the States, given their accent, but they both had a hint of twang that didn't scream the Golden Coast.

"Oh, how funny," she said, noting the location was near the firm where Abby and Jordan worked, RoboTech. "I live just outside of Marin."

Lizzie clapped her hands. "So, we've traveled halfway around the world to meet someone who only lives thirty minutes away?"

"Small world," the husband said and extended a hand. "I'm Sam. It's nice to meet you . . ."

"Cecilia," she supplied. "Nice to meet you, too. And it's

lovely scenery all the same," she said to Lizzie. "I hope you and your boys have a fabulous trip. I'm sure we'll see each other around."

"Text me!" Lizzie whispered as they departed the shuttle. "We can do a spa day! I need some girl time."

CeCe couldn't help smiling at Lizzie's energy. There was something incredibly infectious about her, like a little old granny whom nobody could deny anything. "I will," she whispered back.

Then she gathered her suitcase, which had been delivered to the London hotel overnight, and pulled it in the direction of registration. Thirty minutes later, she was on her way to her very own glass-roofed cabin.

And it was *ah*-mazing.

The first thing CeCe did was drop her bag on the floor and hurry over to the window-encased dome at the end of the cabin. A bed sat beneath the glass, and she jumped on top of it to stare up at the sky. Though it was still daytime, it was already getting dark.

Would this be the night that she saw the aurora borealis?

Hopefully. But maybe not. She at least had time. *Lots* of time, and she would see them, dammit.

For once in her life, one of her dreams was going to come true.

Sighing at the oh-so-lovely thought, she pushed off the bed and set about hanging up her jacket and tucking away her clothes. Then she cranked up the sauna—her cabin had a private one—because that seemed like a very Finnish thing to do.

Later she would walk over to the restaurant for dinner before double-checking the forecast.

Solar activity was predicted to be low for the next few days, but CeCe didn't plan on letting that stop her.

She'd tape her eyelids open if necessary.

Her clothes ended up in a pile near the bed, but she didn't bother picking them up. She could be messy for once and not worry that she would potentially be setting a bad example for her charges.

Naked, she strode toward the sauna and had just sat on the wooden bench, ladle of water in her hand, ready to dump over the hot rocks, when there was a knock on the door.

"Dammit," she muttered and spooned the water onto the rocks before standing and reaching for a towel that was hanging outside the door. It was probably a staff member, having forgotten to tell her something important.

The steam hit her skin and beads of moisture slid down her chest, between her breasts and lower, between her thighs.

She was hot and wet all over, but that had been a common problem of hers of late.

"Seriously," she muttered and headed for the door, throwing it open without glancing through the peephole.

Which was *seriously* an idiotic thing to do.

Because standing on the other side of the door wasn't a staff member with a forgotten bit of advice or a slightly pesky query.

Nope.

Standing on the opposite side of the pane of wood was none other than Colin McGregor.

And she, Cecilia Thiele, idiot of all idiots, lost her grip on her towel.

THIRTEEN

Colin

COLIN'S EYES bugged out of his head for a second, his gaze traveling every inch of CeCe's lush body— gently swaying breasts, narrow hips, flat stomach . . . flaming red curls.

Holy fucking shit.

Then he blinked and realized that any person walking by Cecilia's cabin would be able to see that gorgeous body.

The body that should be for *his* eyes only.

Yes, he was an arrogant asshole. Yes, he knew that Cecilia was a woman and it was technically *her* body first and foremost.

But fuck if Colin wanted another lecherous prick to lay eyes on her.

"Can I come in?" he asked, his voice sounding as though he'd swallowed a bloody flamethrower. He'd called in a favor to an acquaintance that specialized in hacking to find out CeCe's cabin number, had been all the more thankful for that small victory when he'd driven onto the huge property belonging to the resort.

In the meantime, Cecilia was still frozen in shock, her

mouth gaping in a way that made him want to kiss her senseless, so he picked up the towel, wrapped it around her and pushed her gently backward.

Her feet moved without protest, allowing him to step forward into the room. She didn't do *anything* without protest, so Colin knew she was thrown completely for a loop. She didn't speak a word when he closed the door behind him, didn't say anything when he brushed by her to set his bag near the closet. Hell, she didn't even comment when he set the bag of takeaway he'd grabbed from the restaurant on the counter of the little kitchenette tucked away in one corner of the cabin.

In fact, the only thing that seemed to startle her out of her stupor was him dropping his pants to the floor.

"Col—" she began but gasped when his underwear joined the pile.

His socks were next, stuffed into the boots Joanne had sent along with a suitcase of warm clothes, followed by his jacket and shirt.

And then he walked toward Cecilia, wanting nothing more than to strip the towel from her hands before tossing her onto the bed and making love to her under the darkening sky.

But she'd been in the middle of something when he'd knocked.

Colin intended that she finish it *and* was fully committed to naked reciprocity.

He'd seen hers. It was only fair she saw his.

Okay, that wasn't the *only* reason.

He worked out a lot and knew his body was in shape. If seeing him parade around naked somehow convinced CeCe to transform into one of those crazed women at a *Magic Mike* show, then he was all for it.

Yes, he was well aware he was a fool, but a man had to be cognizant of his shortcomings.

A narrow hall opened into a bathroom, but the water wasn't running, and the telltale humidity of an interrupted shower was absent. He closed the door behind him and opened the next, feeling the gust of heat spread over his skin on a rush.

A sauna. Of course.

When in Finland.

"What are—?" Cecilia began from behind his left shoulder, but she didn't get to finish the question because he merely wrapped his fingers around her wrist and tugged her toward the open door.

"Let's finish your sauna," he said, sitting on the bench. "It was rude of me to interrupt."

"As if you give a damn about interrupt—"

He ladled a spoonful of water onto the heated rocks, cutting off what would no doubt have been a scathing remark about his insensitivity.

"Colin!" she exclaimed over the hissing stones and steam filling the air.

"What?" he asked innocently.

"Oh, my God," she said, exasperated. "You're still the same."

"No." He placed his hand over hers, leaning close to stare into her eyes. He needed her to see, needed her to understand that this was their chance at a fresh start, and that he wasn't the same moronic asshole from their past. "I'm not, sweetheart. I've changed. For the better. My family doesn't control me, not any longer." Her fingers pulsed beneath his, startled. "I don't know what happened with them, what they did to you. But I should have known better than to believe them when they said you ran off with Ewan. You're kind, CeCe. Honest, compassionate. You wouldn't do that to me."

Colin's chest was heaving, and his palms were damp . . . and not from the heat of the sauna.

He had to make her understand. He—

"No," she said. "I didn't run off with Ewan." She slipped her hand free of his, pressed it firmly to her chest, just above the towel she still wore. "But I *did* leave with him. It's only . . ." She hesitated, and then sighed deeply. "Ewan gave me an escape route after you shattered my heart into a million pieces."

FOURTEEN

Cecilia

NOW THAT THE time to confront Colin was here, she found it hard to focus.

Maybe that was from shock—how was he here?

Maybe it was because she'd watched him strip naked and just let it happen, enjoying the show.

Stupid.

As in, she was. Yes, the view was great. But attraction to Colin wasn't the problem.

It was all the rest of it. His family. Their breakups. The person she'd become with him. Bending and bending and bending until she'd no longer resembled the woman she wanted to be.

But . . . she was different now.

And she wanted answers, naked or not.

"Why are you here now? After all this time?" Cecilia asked into the silence that descended in the wake of her admission. Her apparent heartbreak had come as a shock, based on Colin's expression of pure horror. Which just further confirmed what she knew in her heart.

This was a tangled mess, one they'd both tangled more by not sitting down and talking.

If she could only go back and kick her twenty-year-old self into action.

She'd corner Lana and Bridget, demand they admit they were trying to break up her and Colin, and then she'd confront Colin himself, tell him what he'd said was absolutely horrendous and unacceptable.

And *then* she would float off into the sunset, her answers found, her pride restored.

No. More. Weaklings.

"I—" He stood, closed the door to the sauna, and sat back down next to her, naked except for a small hand towel tossed haphazardly over his . . .

Penis, Cecilia Thiele, her mind shouted. *It's his penis, and it's giant and glorious and you want to lick it like a lollipop!*

She forced her eyes up and focused on his face, but then got sidetracked by the little scar above his lip and then by his lips themselves. They were yummy and lush and just so flipping kissable. What kind of universe gave a man a mouth like that?

And then he had to go and talk.

To be sweet and make his words both simple and heart-wrenching.

"Because, sweetheart, I couldn't stay away."

"Dammit," she muttered, glancing up at the ceiling, studying the single bulb hanging from the paneled wood. Condensation had gathered on the glass, and the drops sparkled as the light shone through. The effect was beautiful, even though it was slightly blurry through the lens of her tears.

Except, she was trying to channel Heather or Bec, here. To be strong and kickass.

No. She was channeling *herself.*

Maybe her inner strength wasn't so loud or overt, maybe his words called to that hole inside of her, tempting her to just put the past behind her and jump the man and glorious, naked penis.

But that wouldn't solve her problems.

Her mind was getting clearer. Her confidence was growing.

But . . . she still had work to do.

Case in point was not avoiding the conversation with Colin by thinking about anything and everything except what they needed to discuss.

It was just that he sounded so genuine, and she wanted nothing more than to believe that he wanted her. But, how could she?

And yet . . . maybe he did?

No. Part of her couldn't help but think that people didn't change, not truly, not deep down, and though he might want her now, that would inevitably change, and then he would push her away, and she would end up broken all over again.

She *couldn't* end up broken again.

"But why, Col? What do you want?" she asked.

His blue eyes were pained. "I . . . I know what I'm going to give you are just words, and that they're not nearly enough. I know I must have hurt you badly, but I can't remember anything from those days."

Her throat went tight, and she tried to speak, but he covered her hand with his.

"I'm so sorry I hurt you. It was . . . inexcusable to do that to the woman I loved, and I'm so fucking sorry it took me years to grow up and understand that being a man didn't mean taking what I wanted or threatening or proving my dick was big." His fingers convulsed. "I thought I was all grown up, but, in truth, I didn't know a damned thing."

She dropped her chin to her chest. "But what's changed Colin? We're still the same people inside. Yes, we're attracted to each other, but I'm not convinced that we're good in a relationship. I've taken very few leaps in my life, and they've ended up blowing up in my face every time." A sharp shake of her head. "I can't regret them, can't regret the good times I had with you. But I *do* regret the person I was *with* you."

Hurt flickered across his face, but to his credit, his voice was calm when he asked, "Why?"

CeCe sighed. "Because I was weak. Because you loved me, and I loved you so desperately, and I wanted this fairytale to work out." She blinked up at the ceiling again. "But that's not real life. One person can't give and give and *give* while the other takes. *I* can't be that person again."

"I'm not asking you to," he said. "I just want another chance to make things work. For me to be able to prove to you—"

She pulled her hand back.

"I *can't*," she said, shaking her head when he went to reach for her. "I can't do this, Colin. I can't hurt this much and have all this regret and pain and angst. My life is supposed to finally be about me. I need to find out who I am without my job and the remains of our relationship hanging over me. Without my parents' disappointment weighing me down. I need to—"

"I understand." He scooted closer, took her hand in his again. "I get not knowing who you are and your whole world imploding. The fallout from my father's death aside, I've spent the last few months in the same perpetual cycle—thinking I understand how my life revolved, but then recognizing that maybe I didn't know anything at all." He touched her cheek. "I'm different now. I've grown. I know I still have work to do, but I'm not the same stubborn asshole who thinks his shit is made of gold."

His words tempted. His earnestness made that hole in her heart seem a little smaller.

Then he kept talking.

And some of the anger she'd banked over the years flew to the front of her emotions.

"I understand that you were hurt, and I'm sorry that—"

Sweat trickled down between her breasts when she shot to her feet. "No, you *don't* understand," she snapped, "because you weren't the one left shattered. You weren't the one who was devastated when all you'd hoped for a future was fucking *gone*."

He was quiet for a long moment, eyes on hers, the blue unfathomable.

Then he stood and cracked the door, reaching for a robe and handing it to her then repeating the process for himself.

When they were both covered, he brushed his knuckles over her cheek. "You weren't the only one devastated, CeCe. I thought you'd left me for my best friend and then just a month later, my father was dead, the business was one wrong decision away from collapse. I was in over my head. I was scared and . . . you were gone." His voice tightened. "You can't say I was unaffected because I *was*. My life was fucking broken, too."

Her breath caught as the truth of his words hit home. Her anger faded. "I-I'm sorry. I know I should have handled things differently. I should have demanded an explanation, not run off because I was hurt."

"We both shared in the immaturity and stupidity."

She wrinkled her nose, knowing it was true, but still hating it all the same. "Yeah."

Maybe she could convince Heather to invest in time machines and go back six years to give herself and Colin a sharp smack on the forehead.

Silence stretched between them as they stared at each other. She didn't know exactly what to say. Part of her felt better, part of her felt worse, and looking into Colin's blue eyes, seemingly filled with longing, made an answering yearning rise within her.

As stupid as they'd both been, she wanted to go back to those easy times. Back to the hikes on the cliffs, to sketching until the sun went down, to the picnic lunches packed by Joanne and the rides on his horse, the kissing, and . . . more.

If only they could go back.

If only they could forget the past.

But life wasn't that easy. Or at least *hers* wasn't. And as much as she wanted to, she couldn't just put the pain aside and pretend everything between them hadn't happened. She ached and burned and *hurt*. But maybe . . .

Maybe they could move forward.

Maybe she could find a way to give them both a chance to figure out if they could have something healthy . . . together.

"Col?" she asked, when all he did was continue to stare at her. "What are you doing?"

"I'm memorizing every detail of your face so that when you kick me out into the bloody cold Finnish weather, I'll remember that you have a freckle just beneath your left eye and another on the top corner of your lip. I'll remember exactly the way your eyes curve near their corners and how your top lashes are thicker than the bottoms. I'll remember the hint of pink"—he swiped a finger over both of her cheekbones—"just here and here. I'll remember every part of you for the rest of my life. I let the details get blurred in the past, and while I couldn't ever hope to forget you, at least now I'll be able to remember you as perfect as you are in this moment."

Her pulse had picked up its pace during his speech, and her skin had gone taut, heating with desire, with embarrassment, with *awe*. "I think that's the most words I've ever heard you say at one time."

One half of his mouth curved. "Probably."

Silence fell between them again. "Do you really notice all of that?"

A nod. "Aye."

She groaned. "No fair busting out the full Scottish accent."

"All's fair in love and war, lass."

CeCe groaned again, but it was to hide the way her heart had skipped a beat at the word *love*. Though truth be told, it skipped another when Colin called her *lass*.

Ugh.

But also, aw.

And also, shit, *shit*, she was really going to do this. "Col—" she began.

"Aye?"

Or something like *it*.

"You're laying it on real thick. But"—she reached up and placed a finger across his lips when he opened his mouth, presumably to protest—"that wasn't what I was going to say." He nipped at her finger, and she jumped back. "Hey! *Behave*." And yet, Cecilia was grinning and felt light for the first time in years. "I was going to say that maybe we could bring the food over to the bed beneath the glass roof, lie down, and—*Colin*! Stop grinning. I was going to say lie down and watch for the aurora borealis."

"Well, that's disappointing." But he grinned and pushed her in the direction of the bed. "Get comfortable, and I'll grab the food."

She curled up and watched the sky grow fully dark, popping grapes and cheese and crackers into her mouth almost as fast as Colin handed them over. They talked, not about the past, but about the places she wanted to visit next.

Paris because the Eiffel Tower and the Louvre were a must.

Copenhagen because her grandfather had lived there, and

she wanted to visit the palaces and see the colorful buildings next to the harbor.

The Alps. Barcelona. The Colosseum. Maybe Fiji and Malta and Indonesia, somewhere warm and tropical when the weather got cold.

And then back to London.

Because Buckingham Palace and old English manors and changeable weather and small twisting streets surrounded by tall buildings.

And also, she thought, her heart catching when the sky lit up with a magical green hue, back to London because it was closer to a confusing, sweet Scottish man who'd stolen a piece of her heart and had never given it back.

FIFTEEN

Colin

CECILIA MADE the most adorable sounds when she slept—soft mewls as she cuddled closer, gentle sighs that tickled the side of his throat.

She was as beautiful up close as from a distance, and though they'd stayed up late into the night, waiting on the aurora borealis and then finally seeing that distinct glimmer of green light up the dark sky, Colin hadn't allowed himself to sleep.

He was waiting for the other shoe to fall.

He was waiting for Cecilia to see sense.

He needed for her to be more attached to him before it happened. He needed her to love him.

As he'd never stopped loving her.

She yawned and turned in the circle of his arms, stretching and pressing her ass back against his crotch. He tried to shift slightly, so she didn't rub against the giant problem threatening to burst free of the underwear he'd slipped on before they'd settled into bed, but he didn't move quickly enough.

Lights flashed behind his lids, and he hissed out a breath as those luscious curves slid against his cock.

"Fuck," he muttered, placing a hand on CeCe's hip to stay her motions.

"Mmm," she murmured, slipping free and sliding closer.

And, he might as well be honest, it felt so fucking good that he didn't try very hard to keep her away.

"CeCe, baby," he began, but groaned when the soft cushion of her ass tucked right against his erection. Fuck, but she felt good against him.

"Mmm," she murmured again and then went ramrod stiff.

Shit. Colin tensed, preparing to haul his ass out into the cold.

She rolled over and opened her eyes, those green irises startlingly clear. One hand reached up to cup his cheek. "I thought it was a dream," she said softly.

"Not a dream." He turned his head and pressed a kiss to her palm. "Did you know your eyes are the same color as the northern lights?"

One half of her mouth curved. "Really?"

He kissed that curve. "Aye."

She shuddered and he smirked. "Still not playing fair, are you?"

"When it comes to you?" he asked, not giving her a chance to reply. "Never." Another kiss. "I'll never play fair when it comes to winning you back, sweetheart. Letting you go was the biggest mistake—*mistakes*—of my life."

She smiled and it lit up the room. Or maybe that was his heart. "I like it when you don't play fair."

Then that smile faltered and the brightness faded. He tried to figure out the underlying meaning of her words, why they'd hurt her so much.

"You—" he began.

But he didn't get the chance to finish the sentence because then Cecilia's mouth was on his and her hand was on his cock and . . . his head was spinning.

He pulled back. "Wait, baby. What—"

She sat up, tearing off the robe she'd fallen asleep in, and fuck but she was more gorgeous than ever. "Do you want me, Colin? Because I *need* you to make me feel good. I need you to make me forget that we were only together the once. I need you to help me forget what came after."

"I don't think that—" He shook his head. "We need to talk. We shouldn't just bury—"

"Then just get the *fuck* out!" she screamed. "Because you're going to leave anyway, and then I'll be broken again, and I can't. I wanted to and I thought I could, but *I can't.*" She shoved off the bed, snatching the robe and trying to wrestle it on as she ran.

Which didn't go well.

Colin saw her start to go down before she realized what was happening, saw the tie of the robe tangled around her ankles as she started to sprint down the hall.

He moved, not thinking, not trying to process the words nor the frustration he felt for not knowing what the fuck was going on.

"Ah!" CeCe stumbled and went down in a jumble of limbs.

But he was there.

He caught her.

As he should have done all those years ago.

He righted her, tugged the robe over her shoulders, and tied it snugly around her waist. She wouldn't look at him, but he didn't need to see her eyes to know they were shimmering with tears.

"Right, then," he said, as he should have in the past. "We're not leaving here until we have both said all there is to say."

Her chin came up, and her eyes went cold. "I can leave here whenever I want."

Fuck. She could. And he had no fucking right to demand anything from this woman. "You can," he said. "*Of course,* you can."

She scoffed, didn't look at him.

"But, sweetheart, I don't want you to go," he said. "I've spent years feeling empty, years being a fucking idiot, years knowing I'd lost you, that I lost the absolute best thing in my life."

Her lips parted. Her eyes squeezed closed. "I can't do this again, Colin. I fell for you after high school and then you broke my heart. I fell again after I got hurt, was barely picking up the pieces of my life when you barreled in and won my trust, despite my best efforts to keep you away." She shoved back her hair with a shaking hand. "And then you left me at the altar, and when I called you on the phone to find out why you weren't there, you said horrible things th-that shattered me into even smaller pieces. I—" Her exhale was shaky. "I can't do that again."

Joanie's words paired with CeCe's, and his throat went tight as the truth settled on his heart, heavier than ever. Fuck, he'd known he'd done something wrong. But he didn't realize it was this *horribly* wrong.

And he couldn't fucking remember.

For a second, that old darkness, the immaturity and ego, threatened to well up. To demand she give him the explanation he deserved. To convince her she would be stupid to not just immediately forgive him.

Then, just as quickly, it passed.

He'd grown and changed and become a better person. If he wanted a shot with this wonderful woman, he needed to show her that the change was real and permanent.

"I don't want there to be any more secrets or pain," he said. "I want to move on."

"I don't know," she whispered. "It's not that easy to just close the chapter and move forward."

He knew that. But he also knew that he needed this woman in his life. "I want to understand exactly what happened, and I want you to understand what *I* thought happened. At a minimum, I think we both need that." He placed both hands on her shoulders. "We've run long enough. We've let circumstances and our families manipulate us. But we're not young or naïve or gullible anymore. We can have the truth. The *full* truth."

He sucked in a breath when she finally looked at him, and the force of her pain socked him in the gut. Her words were equally as impactful. "I'm not sure I want it."

No. She had to. Otherwise—

Inhaling, he forced himself to calm, to speak from the heart. "From the moment I met you on that hillside, red hair flowing behind you as you corralled that horse"—a beast of a horse that had belonged to his sister—"I knew we had a connection." Colin clenched his jaw, regret pouring through him all over again. "I didn't trust in it like I should have. I wasn't strong enough to treat you as you deserved. I understand that. Just as I understand and will abide by your wishes if you want me to go."

He'd go if she asked.

But he wouldn't stay away. He'd find a way to make things right. No matter what.

She swallowed. "He was scared."

He touched her jaw. "Me or Ab?"

Ab being the horse that had belonged to his sister. The horse that brought a smile to CeCe's lips for a brief moment before it was gone like so much smoke, before quiet descended, a long, stretched-out silence that scoured his skin.

When she finally spoke, her voice was gentle. "For a long

time, I assumed it was just Ab." Green eyes on his, holding his gaze, prompting him to speak.

"I did, too," he said, cupping her cheek. "But the truth is that I was terrified. I was trying so hard to be the man my father wanted, the one my family demanded. I locked all my extra emotions away and pushed them down after we were over until I wasn't sure I would ever be able to feel anything again." He sighed. "Maybe you're right, maybe we wouldn't have worked out because I didn't have the strength to be the husband you deserved." He let his hand fall from her face. "But I loved you, and I searched for you, sweetheart, and seeing you again, now, after all this time, I know that I want to try to make things right between us." Unable to stop touching her for long, not when she was in front of him, not when the giant cavern in his chest was finally beginning to be filled in, he brushed a lock of hair off her forehead. "So, I guess the question is, do you want me to try and make things right? Do you want something—a relationship, *more*, that might be *us* again?"

She sucked in a breath, her eyes closing for so long that his gut twisted into knots, and then those knots twisted into more knots.

"It wouldn't have to be an us," he said when it seemed she wouldn't speak, or worse, when the answer might be no. "Or at least not the *us* from before. We could build something stronger. We could have more." He braced himself for her refusal, even as the words kept coming. "I'm stronger now. I know my family isn't the perfect entity I'd made them out to be. I've seen their manipulation—"

Her eyes flashed with hurt, and his heart sank like a stone.

"That's it, isn't it?" he asked gently. "They did something to you."

"Col—" She broke off, shook her head.

He squeezed her fingers. "I know they were good at manipulating me to get what they wanted, but that's changed. I don't let them do that anymore, and I haven't for some time," he added. "If you give me this chance, I won't let anyone or anything come between us."

More silence. Longer this time. And the longer it went on, the more clearly he felt the pain of her rejection lick up his spine.

She was going to say no.

And he'd deserve it.

Because even without all the details, he could see the hurt, knew that whatever had made her leave with Ewan was grievous.

"I've grown up, CeCe," he said. "I won't hurt you. Not ever again."

She was still and quiet, so damned quiet. But as he studied her closely, Colin watched the pain in her eyes fade, saw the thread of hope faintly creep in on their edges.

And for a heartbeat, he dared to hope.

"Technically," she whispered, "that was two questions."

"Pardon?" His brows drew together, hope displaced by confusion.

"Before," she whispered. "You asked two questions—do I want you to make things right? Yes, I *do* want you to make things right. But . . . I also want to make *my* part in this right. Because I made mistakes, too. I'm not perfect. I should have—" A shake of her head, a sigh. Then she smiled, small and tentative, but it was there, as was the fire in her expression, the determination. His pulse slowed. Those knots untangled. "As for the other question—do I maybe want to be an *us* again?—the answer to that is—" Her teeth pressed into her bottom lip, released after a moment. "Yes. And I know it's probably stupid, that I should turn in my feminist card. But . . . I missed you. I miss what we had. I want to see what we might be, now that we've grown up."

"I'll make it up to you," he promised. "I'll make things right." He didn't miss the flicker of uncertainty in her eyes, knew that it would take time for her to trust him again. "Now," he said, trying to sound casual but no doubt failing horribly at it, "is this a tea or a whiskey conversation?"

Silence. Another bout of the tense quiet.

Then she grinned, laughing when they both answered at the same time, "Whiskey. Definitely whiskey."

SIXTEEN

Cecilia

"I DON'T REALLY KNOW where to begin," CeCe said, whiskey in hand. She took a sip of the fiery liquid, relishing the burn as it went down, soaking up the notes of oak and honey and—

She was delaying.

But she really didn't know where to start.

The image of him walking away on the cliff side eight years before, the wind mussing his hair, the moonlight transforming his solid form into shadows in mere seconds had broken a piece of her CeCe knew would never be the same.

Her innocence.

No, *that* part had been freely given. But even though they'd gotten back together two years later, their first breakup had stripped her of her emotional innocence, had dismantled her ability to . . . dream.

Happy endings were no longer guaranteed. She wouldn't ever be rescued by a man on a white—or in his case, a *black* —stallion.

It had taken her a long time before she'd begun to appreciate that having her heart broken had ultimately been a good thing. She couldn't have continued in this world with those naïve, rose-colored glasses on. She certainly wouldn't have survived college if not for Colin's cold treatment.

And she probably never would have spoken to him again at all if he hadn't messaged at one of her lowest times.

A torn rotator cuff.

A hugely significant tear that had required surgery.

She remembered being helped into a sling by the sports therapist, Sally, pain scorching her left arm with each tiny adjustment, but that hurt had been eclipsed by the conversation echoing through the closed door to her coach's office when he'd phoned her parents to tell them of her injury.

The voice that had been alternately stunned then shocked into silence then furious when her coach told her parents she'd been injured.

"What do you mean, it serves her right?" he'd shouted, making her wince and Sally apologize for hurting her.

CeCe hadn't the heart to tell Sally that her shoulder was nothing when compared to knowing that her parents were cold-hearted assholes, who just couldn't put their own egos aside to love their daughter as she was.

It had been stupid to hope, to dream that her parents might one day see reason and find a way to care for her.

But that wasn't possible.

Then Colin had messaged while she was hurt, and hadn't stopped messaging, even when she ignored him. He'd pestered her until she finally knew she would either have to block him or respond . . . and she'd been so lonely and so distraught by the agonizing recovery process, by her parent's estrangement that she'd finally sent something back. Of course, it had taken approximately two point six million emails and DMs from Colin before she'd even begun to forgive him.

But he'd been there. And he'd been her only constant.

They'd first rebuilt their friendship over long online chats about anything but her shoulder, her family—she'd wanted to forget her injury, what her parents had done. So instead, they'd spent most of their time discussing TV and movies, their likes and dislikes, the things they'd wanted to do together in her free time. They'd stolen moments in between all her couch surfing, around her hectic schedule as she'd worked any job she could muster in order to pay her medical bills—everything from fast food to contract drawing work.

But she'd never reached out to her parents again. Not after the surgery, not after the physical therapy, not after all the blood, sweat, and tears had left her with a shoulder that would never be good enough to swim competitively again.

God, how her shoulder had hurt, and, *God*, how the bills had piled up.

She'd lost her scholarship with the college, along with her health insurance.

But eventually she'd been able to get caught up enough to rent a room, and then later when their friendship had once again turned into something more, when because of his support, CeCe had been able to move past the hurtful relationship with her parents, to tuck it away and push forward and work harder, she had accepted his offer to stay with him in Scotland.

What more had she to lose?

Of course, if she'd known how much more she *could* lose, she would have never gone back.

Yay for hindsight.

But also yay for growing up, for no longer running from her problems.

Warm fingers brushed her cheek. "I don't care where you start, sweetheart. Just tell me *anything*."

She sighed and glanced down at the glass in her hand, running one finger over the curved edge. "I think, if you hadn't messaged me again right at the moment you did six years ago, I wouldn't have come back to Scotland, wouldn't have wanted to start over with you. No matter what."

"I wouldn't have stopped." A pause, blue eyes locked on hers. "*No matter what.*"

Her lips twisted. "You say that so confidently."

"I almost flew over when I found out you'd been hurt."

"What?" She glanced up and saw the truth in his eyes. "Why didn't you?"

He took a sip of whiskey. "I didn't think I'd be welcomed by your parents, and I didn't think it would be good for your recovery to have me there, mucking things up."

The sky outside was already beginning to darken, the hours of daylight being swallowed up as easily as krill into a blue whale's mouth.

CeCe thought of all the times she'd skirted his questions about her parents, where she was living, why she was working so much after recovering from a major surgery, and she wished again that she'd had it within her all those years ago to communicate effectively.

She'd held all the wrong things in. She'd made so many childish mistakes.

Then again . . . she'd been a *child*.

But she was grown now, and she sure as hell wasn't going to do the same damned thing. She was going to be better, to demand more of herself, of Colin. "I wish you would have come."

He held her gaze. "Me, too."

Tilting her head back to stare up at the ceiling, she took a few moments to gather her thoughts.

"So, you know I got hurt. I'd had a great season after"—she straightened and gestured between the two of them—"after *us*."

"You told me you had a real shot at Nationals," he said.

"Yes," she agreed, "I thought the possibilities were endless from there. International competitions, maybe the Olympics, who knew, but things were looking really good. I was swimming faster, had never been in better shape." She took another sip. "And that continued over the summer. I swam every day and worked two jobs, since my scholarship didn't cover me for the non-school months. But that meant I didn't get out of shape and had an okay amount of money saved by the time school started."

"But then you got hurt," he said. "You never wanted to talk about exactly how it happened."

The memory still stung, one of those perpetual *if onlys*, but she went through it again, needed him to understand that it had framed so much of her thinking at the time. "It was in the first competition of the season. I felt something tear but kept swimming because it was in the final stretch of the race. I won." CeCe shook her head. "Turns out, if I hadn't pushed through the pain, I might still have a racing career."

Colin took the empty glass from her hand and set it on the table. "You couldn't have known that."

She shrugged. "A fact I understand *now*, but one that also haunted me for a good long while."

He brushed his knuckles across her cheek. "How long did it haunt you, sweetheart?"

"Frankly?"

A nod.

"It *still* bothers me," she said with a huff. "But you can't go back and change the past. The worst part was my parents never came, never called. Hell, they never even sent a card. Their only daughter's life and she had needed a pretty serious surgery followed by physical therapy, but they never once came to check on me."

"You never told me that."

"It was easier to forget," she said. "And avoid." Her eyes met his. "I'm really good at both of those, in case you haven't noticed."

He stroked a hand down her arm. "And *I'm* good at not seeing what's in front of me, at ignoring problems because I don't want to create conflict." Blue eyes flashed. "It's fucked up. If only—"

"We'd done things differently," she said softly.

"Yes." He swallowed hard. "That."

CeCe's eyes burned, but she felt the edges of those jagged wounds close slightly, their ache easing enough that she could breathe a little easier.

Colin touched her cheek. "I'm sorry about your parents."

She shrugged, her voice resigned. "That's the way they are. It just took until after my injury for me to truly understand they would never change. And, truthfully, I'd broken something in them, too. I wasn't their perfect daughter. I didn't stay close to home and go to the college they'd decided on for me. I didn't marry the man they'd chosen and start popping out kids. I wanted to travel and draw and swim fast." She laced her fingers together, pressing them to her heart. "I wanted to live my own life, and that would never *ever* be compatible with their expectations."

"It's their loss," Colin said fiercely, brushing back a strand of her ponytail that was lying around her throat. "I know I'm far from innocent in this, that I fucked up royally, but I don't know how a parent could do that to a child."

"I know." She laughed, and it sounded broken. "We both really got screwed in the parental department. I mean, I got disowned because I wanted to take a trip I was paying for myself and then swim competitively a few states away from home, and your mother—"

Colin straightened, eyes going flinty and cold. "What did my mother do to you?"

"Well, it was more to you." CeCe opened and closed her mouth. Damn, she hadn't wanted to go about it this way. She didn't want to hurt him, and her next words would *definitely* hurt him. "Though I guess you could say it was to *us*—"

The trill of her phone cut through her words.

She reached for it.

He stopped her. "Don't."

"I have to." She slipped her fingers from beneath his. "It's Hunter's ringtone, and I haven't talked to him yet."

Colin sighed, chin dropping to his chest. "Then, of course, you have to answer it." His tone was sincere, absent of sarcasm, and that settled some of the raging storm inside her.

Cecilia swiped across the screen, a smile breaking out on her lips when Hunter's little face appeared on her phone.

Saved by FaceTime.

That was a new one.

"Bye, CeCe!" Hunter shouted and then disappeared from the screen. A heartbeat later, Abby's face appeared in his place.

"Not you!" CeCe joked. "Where's my little squishy's face?"

Abby laughed but turned the camera around so she could see Carter toddling around the floor, a large plastic truck clutched in one hand. "And I'll have you know he told me just this morning *Carter no squish-squish.*"

"No!" CeCe said, collapsing back onto the bed and

watching the darkening sky through the windows. "He's growing up too fast."

"I know." Abby sighed. "But that's not the only thing that's going to be growing." She pointed at her belly.

"What?" CeCe's jaw dropped open. "Are you saying what I think you're saying?"

Abby nodded. "Yup. Jordan is once again banned from wearing deodorant."

CeCe burst into laughter. "Don't tell me the smell of it is making you sick again!"

Her friend rolled her eyes. "Every freaking type." But then she laughed. "My nose told me I was pregnant before the pregnancy test could."

"Oh, my God."

"I know."

"You're having another baby."

"*I know*." Abby widened her eyes. "What the hell were we thinking?"

CeCe smiled. "That you're good parents?" A beat. "Plus, you have a hell of a nanny."

Abby blew out a breath. "About that . . ."

Cecilia's gut dropped.

"I was wondering if you would consider working for me."

Pregnancy brain was already striking her poor friend. "I *do* work for you, Abs."

She waved a hand. "I'm screwing this up. I meant, I want you to put your art skills to work in my department." Both palms came up. "No pressure, but your drawings are so amazing that I was hoping to hire you as a freelance artist. You could work from here or on your travels. I just . . . you're family, CeCe, and my kids and I are so lucky to have you. But I don't want to be the one to hold you back, not when you're so talented, honey. You deserve to have all your dreams come true."

Cecilia's eyes filled with tears. "Dammit, Abs. You had to go and do it."

Her friend sniffed and wiped a hand across her cheek. "I'm sorry. I mean, *I'm not sorry*. But I'm also a hormonal mess and have been emotionally puking all over everyone." Jordan appeared briefly on the screen, a box of tissues in his hand. He put them in Abby's lap and looked into the phone. "She asked you yet? You're going to say yes, right?"

"Ugh." Abby slapped his arm. "Stop being so pushy, dammit."

"Language." He smacked a kiss to her lips and glanced back at the camera, winking at CeCe. "Yup, she's definitely going to say yes."

"Jordan!"

"*Abigail*." He kissed her again, a little longer than before. "I love you to pieces."

"Congrats," CeCe murmured when he broke away to look into the camera.

He studied her through the screen, eyes concerned. The man was an emotional ninja, somehow always knowing when she'd needed a hug or a break from the stress of Hunter's care. Today was no different. One look and he knew something was up. "You doing okay?"

She nodded. "I'm fine. I just . . . I had some stuff come up."

His brows pulled together. "Do you need me to—?"

"*I'm all right*." CeCe put enough emphasis on the words that Jordan stopped talking and studied her. "If you say so," he said after a moment.

Her lids narrowed. "I *do* say so."

One half of his mouth turned up into a smile. "Okay then. Enjoy your travels, and I'll try to make sure Abby doesn't bug you too much—"

"Hey!" Abby protested.

"Be safe and don't hesitate to call. What?" He glanced off screen and CeCe could hear a female voice shouting something in the background. Rolling his eyes as he turned back, he said, "Apparently, Heather will be in Germany next week and wants me to plan her social calendar for her. She asked me to ask you about possibly getting together if the dates work out."

Jordan's sister, Heather, was another part of their raucous, romance-reading, ridiculously-expensive-pajama-loving quintet. She was also a true ball-buster and really fun to hang out with.

"That would be great. I'll text her."

"Awesome. Enjoy yourself, CeCe." He shifted slightly to the right so Cecilia could see Abby on the screen again. "Say goodbye, sweetheart."

"Wait!" Abby said. "I didn't get to ask if you finished reading the book. Chapter Sixteen has that scene with the—"

Jordan sighed and waved to CeCe. "Bye." Then he bent to kiss Abby again, pressing the button to disconnect the call.

All the noise cut off in a split second, and she sighed into the silence, surprised at how much she missed her friends, Hunter's sweet face, and even Carter's little squishy toddler legs.

They were her family, and she was homesick for them.

Funny how she'd never felt homesick before, but her little motley crew of kids and adults had become more of a real family to her than her own blood.

They were her anchor in the way she'd once hoped Colin would be.

Her breath caught because *Colin*.

As in, she'd forgotten he was in the room with her.

CeCe sat up from the bed and whirled around. He was on the couch, a book in his hand. Her heart was pounding for some reason. No, not for *some* reason. She felt like she'd accidentally shown the table her hand in poker. Okay, that was a terrible analogy, but him overhearing the conversation was almost as though she'd stripped off too many layers of skin and was now a throbbing and vulnerable *and* homesick mess.

Colin looked up from the book. "Your friends seem nice."

The breath she'd been holding slid free. "They're the absolute best."

"*You're* the best." His lips tipped up.

She crossed over to the sitting space and picked up a glass of whiskey—his, hers, she didn't know at this point—and had just lifted it to her lips for a sip when she recognized what he was reading.

What. He. Was. Reading.

"What are you doing?" she gasped.

He turned the page. "She said chapter sixteen, right?" A tilt of his head. "Oh. *Oh.*"

"Colin!" She tried to grab the book from his hands.

"He puts his . . . *what?*"—Colin's eyes went wide—"*where?*"

"Oh. My. God," she muttered. "This is not happening."

"And his tongue? Holy . . ." He trailed off and looked up at her. "You read this?"

Cecilia's cheeks were burning. "Seriously, just stop. Oh, my God." She groaned again when he kept the book out of her reach and still managed to turn another page.

This book was dirtier than the last. A contemporary romance about a boss and his best friend's sister. He was a sex god and really, *really* adventurous in bed. Which was hot when reading it by herself or reflecting on it with her little Energizer Bunny of a vibrator.

It was also critically embarrassing when it was Colin reading about the sex god's . . . *godliness* and then giving her incredulous looks.

"And then he—" Colin dropped the book low enough for her to rip it out of his grip and launch it across the room. She barely heard the *plunk* as it smacked against the floor. Instead, she was suddenly aware of his body beneath hers, of his hard *Scottish broadsword*—to steal a surprisingly fitting term from her historical novels—pressed against her thigh. She was draped over him like a blanket and when he looked at her with heat in his gaze, she couldn't possibly be held responsible for her reaction. "You read that?"

"I'm not innocent any longer."

His eyes heated further. His hands slipped to her waist.

She lost the battle with herself.

Her hands went from his chest to his head. She dropped her mouth down to his.

And she kissed him with all the pent-up heat and emotion and yearning from the last eight years.

SEVENTEEN

Colin

THE WOMAN COULD *KISS*.

Her mouth was urgent yet soft, hurried but somehow giving him the sense that she was still savoring every second.

Colin didn't realize he'd been sitting there frozen, lost in the sensation of CeCe being his arms but not actively participating in her kiss, until his woman pulled back and glared at him. "Kiss me, dammit."

He didn't need to be told twice.

He wrapped his arms around CeCe's waist, and leaned back against the couch cushions.

Curves beneath his fingertips, breasts pressed against his chest, and then skin . . . And *fuck*, yes. Her skin was like velvet, silky smooth, and flushed pink from the blood rushing beneath the surface.

Not that his blood was calm and hanging out below his skin . . . or at least not *all* his skin. It had shifted so it was in a very specific, very hard and aching location.

CeCe shoved at the T-shirt he'd shrugged on when her

phone had rung, not wanting to be half-naked and scarring a child if he happened to get caught on the screen.

But instead of being caught *in flagrante delicto,* he'd been captivated by the voices coming from her phone. Jealous of the easy familiarity between her and her former employer. Touched by how good she'd been with Hunter. She loved those people.

He was glad.

But it also made him ache.

Because he wanted her more.

He wanted this kiss to be about the future more than the past.

He wanted this moment to be the beginning of some magical happily ever after, like in one of her books.

"Colin," she said, tearing her mouth away, her breath coming in short gasps, her hands on his chest, his abs . . . teasing lower. "Your head is working too hard." She grinned. "And not this one," she added with a punctuating pat on his cock.

His hips shot up at the touch, and he groaned. "God, sweetheart. I love your hands on me. But—*ah*—I feel like we should finish the conversation—"

Her hand reached into his boxer briefs and squeezed. Hard. "Fuck now. Talk later."

Considering that Colin's eyes were rolling into the back of his skull, he couldn't argue.

Except, he *had* to argue.

Because somehow, he was lucky enough to have a third chance with the woman he loved, and he could not afford to fuck it up.

"CeCe." He gathered his wits, pulled her hand from his pants, and yanked her so she was flush against him. Which almost shredded his already tenuous control, because she was soft to his hard, smelled so damned amazing, and when she undulated against him—

Fuck, he wanted her.

Except . . . Cecilia might be determined to live in the moment, to pretend the past didn't still have its claws in him, but he knew they couldn't do this, not yet anyway.

Not without them both understanding *exactly* what had happened six years before.

"Stop," he said. "Sweetheart, *just stop.*"

CeCe finally froze, though her chest heaved, and her green eyes gleamed with pain. "I just want to forget," she said, tears leaking out of the corners of her eyes. "I just want to move on."

He wiped away that glistening moisture, pressed a soft kiss to her lips.

Then he waited.

Her first instinct was always to run, but he couldn't let her. Not this time. Not when it meant their future.

Luckily, his patience paid off.

Glassy emerald eyes met his, and her exhale was shaky. "I don't want to hurt you."

God, she undid him.

"Haven't we hurt each other enough?" he asked softly. "We've let the past come between us, the secrets chip away at everything that's held us together. We both need to know *everything.*"

A nod before her chin dropped to her chest. "You're right."

"So, tell me, sweetheart. Please."

Another shuddering breath. "Okay." One more shaking inhale and exhale. "Okay." Her gaze met his. "What do you remember from that day?"

He closed his eyes, tugging at the swirling twisted memories. He'd gotten up and dressed in his kilt, knowing that CeCe would love it, and then his mother and sister had come in with . . . "My mom showed me your journal. You'd written"—he swallowed against the hurt those words, in her own hand, had wrought. "You said you coming to Scotland, taking me back—" A shake of his head. "You'd written that your forgiveness after our first breakup was all a ruse, a way to pay me back for hurting you. You said I was just a pawn and you were going to wring every pound out of me then break my heart in revenge—" He broke off, opened his eyes.

"I didn't," she said and shifted so she was sitting beside him instead of on his lap. "Lana"—his sister—"had borrowed a journal. Ewan told me that one of her friends, Olivia, used to forge notes for you in school. He thought she'd done it, especially"— one half of her mouth curved into a bittersweet smile—"because I've never referred to a vacation as a holiday or a trunk of a car as a bonnet or even a shopping cart as a trolley . . ." She trailed off with a shrug. "A lot of things were off about the journal. But perhaps, you had to be me or at least an American, anyway, to see the word choice was completely wrong."

His throat had tightened the more CeCe talked. Because, of course, she was right. His family hadn't wanted him to marry Cecilia—both because she was American and also because she wasn't the woman they'd chosen for him . . . Olivia.

Olivia had been a neighbor, Lana's closest friend, and she'd also had a crush on him since they were children.

And Olly *was* beautiful, but she was also weak and went along with everything Lana said. There was also the fact that his mother and sister had thrown them together more times than he could count after the botched wedding.

Not that he'd been having any of that. He'd been too heart-broken and devastated—

Fuck.

If only he'd taken a moment—

He should have taken a *fucking* moment.

"But it wasn't just the journal, Col," she asked, resting one hand on his shoulder. "Was it?"

He shook his head.

Her expression softened. "See? And this is part of *my* regret, of wishing I did something, *anything* different. Instead, I got hurt and I ran. I hate that I did that"—a sigh—"that I *still* do that. I want to be kick ass, like my friends. To be tough and strong. To push back and demand. But all I ever seem to do is run to avoid conflict." Haunted green eyes drifted to his, made his heart convulse.

"No," he said. "This is all *my* fault. I'm such a fucking idiot. I believed them. How could I have believed them?" He shoved a hand through his hair, yanking at the strands. He'd known letting her go was the worst mistake of his life, but knowing why —that'd he'd thrown it all out over a few forged words, made it infinitely worse.

"Col—"

He locked his eyes with hers. "Will you give me another chance, sweetheart?" he asked. "I know I don't deserve it, but I'm asking—no, I'm begging you to let me prove to you that I've changed."

"Col—"

He touched her cheek. "And, if you give me this chance and we fight or something goes wrong and you run, know I'll find you," he said. "Know I won't stop looking, that I won't give up. And if someday you're done with me, if you want to break my heart, it'll be on a silver platter for you. Always. Forever."

"I don't want to hurt you, baby," she whispered.

"I know." He touched her chest, just above her heart. "Because even though the world, even though *I've* done my best to scar this"—he tapped the spot lightly—"it's pure. It's filled with love and joy and sweetness, and that's part of what makes you so fucking impressive."

Colin knew the words weren't exactly the most elegant or romantic. But they had to be said. And he'd say them to her over and over and *over* again until she began to believe him. She had to believe that she was special. That she was important and valuable—

Six years of damage. *No.* Longer than that. He'd broken her heart when she was eighteen, when he'd fallen for her but had been too scared of disappointing his parents to fight for her. The irony was that CeCe thought she was weak, but she was the strongest woman he knew. She'd fought for her independence, had gained it at great cost. And she'd never looked back.

That was strength.

What Colin had done in turn—catering to the demands of his parents—was the personification of pathetic.

"And you're not weak," he said, knowing she needed the words, better words, and wanting to give them to her, wanting her to see herself as *he* saw her. "You didn't become your parents' puppet. You fought through a serious injury. You survived a broken heart—twice." He cupped her cheek. "And built a life for yourself. With wonderful people who see your value. Who love you." He brushed his thumb lightly over her skin. "You did good."

Her breath shuddered out. "I just did my best," she murmured. "Put my head down and pretended I was fine."

That was such a CeCe thing to say.

To discount and minimize. But she needed to know she'd done something wonderful by not letting the hard, the heartbreaking events stop her from living her life.

"Sweetheart," he said. "I don't *want* you to pretend you're fine. I want to know everything that's in your heart, your mind. I know that we had—we *have*—a connection. I know we had an intense relationship, but I also know we couldn't really talk about the important things. Maybe it was maturity. Maybe I just wasn't able to be the partner you needed." He sucked in a breath, released it slowly. "But I do know I don't want that for you, for us."

Her eyes drifted away. "I don't know if I have the strength to be real." A beat as Colin opened his mouth, a rebuttal on the tip of his tongue, but Cecilia beat him to the punch. She shook her head in one abrupt movement. "No," she said. "Fuck *that*. I'm done being that. I'm done running or being a weakling." She stepped away from him, started to pace. As she moved, she shoved her hands into her hair, shifting the heavy locks, giving him a glimpse of that tattoo on her nape. He now had a crystal-clear understanding of exactly why Hunter was so important to her.

He was so damned proud of what she'd become.

And he was so damned ashamed of how weak he'd been.

She reached the hall, paused, and Colin watched her shoulders rise and fall on a breath.

Then she spun to face him.

"So, if I'm done running, if I'm taking this trip so that I can find myself, so that I can prove I can be strong and mature and valuable then I need to put my money where my mouth is and *stop* running, *stop* being weak, *stop* thinking that just because my parents, because *you* didn't love me the way I deserved, that I don't have value."

God, that hurt.

But she was right. He hadn't valued her or her love. He'd jumped to conclusions and hadn't believed in her.

She'd run. He'd let her go.

Her chin lifted. "Okay, so talk to me. What else went down, because if it had just been the journal, I think we . . ."

"Might have been able to work it out?" he asked, and she nodded. "Yeah. I think you might be right. But it wasn't just the journal. My mother had receipts for expensive clothes and the wedding dress—"

"I didn't ask for—"

He laced his fingers through hers. "I know. *Now*." He cursed, anger once again eating at him. Why hadn't he realized? "But that's no bloody excuse. I should have known then."

"There are a lot of things we both should have done," she said, squeezing his hand before exhaling deeply. "Then the bank account added even more fuel to the fire."

Surprised she knew that piece, Colin's eyes shot to hers.

She nodded. "Ewan told me when he came to confront me at the church. After he realized what was happening, he gave me his phone, had me call you. Do you remember?"

Colin frowned, searching through those memories. "I think so? I started drinking right after they showed me the journal and kept drinking through the receipts, the account, the boxes of wedding china you supposedly *had* to have."

Which was fucking pathetic. He thrust a hand in his hair, spun away, unable to believe that he hadn't just talked to her.

Whiskey. Anger. Not listening. Just like his father.

What a fucking lineage he came from.

But the past wasn't as important as this woman, as understanding and taking ownership. So, he turned back, crossed to her. "What did I say to make you leave?"

A shadow crossed her face. "It doesn't matter."

Every cell in his body filled with ice. Because *this*, this was the truth of what had torn them apart. "It matters, sweetheart," he whispered. "Don't run. Don't pretend it's okay. Just tell me, so we can move on." God, he hoped he could find a way for them to push through because otherwise, it would just hang over them forever.

Tears filled her eyes, but CeCe blinked them away and lifted her chin. "It wasn't a big deal—or, well . . . it isn't *now*. I've moved past it. I'm okay," she said, affecting a casual tone despite him knowing that the memories had to be shredding her inside.

"Sweetheart."

Her gaze went to his, steady and even and . . . filled with old pain. "You insinuated that the events . . ." A sigh. "You said they'd made you understand exactly why my parents had disowned me."

Fuck.

He paced away. "*Fuck!*"

How could he have said such a thing?

What special kind of bastard was he?

"God." He thrust a hand through his hair. "I'm such a fucking—"

Arms wrapped around his waist, a shaky chuckle punctuating the action. "Feel better?"

Shocked laughter burst out of him. "No," he said, turning around so he could take her in his arms. But she'd managed to slightly temper the anger he felt for his own idiotic actions. *Slightly* was the key word there because he knew it would take him a long time for him to forgive himself. What he'd said was unforgiveable. It had taken her softest, most vulnerable spot—that her parents hadn't loved her enough to appreciate her independence, to be there for her even though they didn't want the same things for her life—and exploited it.

He'd purposely chosen the way to hurt her the most.

After he'd won her trust again.

"Damn." She rose on tiptoe, pressed a kiss to his cheek. "Way to kill the mood, McGregor."

He smiled at her joke, but his words were serious. "I will spend every single day for the rest of my life making it up to you."

"No." She shoved at his chest, any trace of amusement fading away. "*No.* You don't get to do that, Colin. You don't get to shoulder everything like it was all your fault. *I* was there, too. I could have done things differently, pushed harder, refused to leave until you knew the truth." She raised her hands then dropped them back at her sides. "I ran. And I shouldn't have."

God, this woman. She was it for him.

Always had been, always would be.

So, when she ended her rant with a firm, "Got it, mister?" he nodded. And when she asked if he wanted to take a walk, he nodded again, got dressed alongside her then grabbed both their coats and helped her into hers.

Colin knew he wouldn't ever be able to deny her anything.

Cecilia Thiele absolutely owned him.

EIGHTEEN

Cecilia

CECE SHRIEKED with joy as they went over a huge dune of snow. Dune? Was that even the correct word? She knew there were sand dunes, but were there *snow* dunes?

Clearly, she'd been out of the Midwest and in California for too long if she couldn't remember the correct term.

Pile?

Drift? Ah, yes! That was it.

They'd gone up and over, their sled bumping to the ground with a jolt that threatened to steal her breath, but then Colin had his arm around her waist, tucking her safely against his side and all the hard muscles there. He was taking his job of keeping her safely in the basket very seriously, so her breathlessness was purely sexy Scot related.

Also, it was fun.

The dogs were barking as they towed the sled forward, little doggy smiles on their mouths, tails bouncing as they ran.

Adorable. If they weren't so noisy, she'd almost want a team for herself.

Yup, that would be *super* practical in California.

Hold on Hunter and Carter, let's jump on the sled and take the dogs down for a Happy Meal at McDonald's.

Totally doable, right?

Colin leaned down, the stubble on his chin teasing the skin behind her left ear. "What are you smiling about?"

She turned her head and spoke directly into his ear, so he could hear her over the barking, knowing she had a giant grin on her face. "How much the kids would love this."

His face softened but his eyes heated, and that space between her thighs, went tight.

And wet.

Which Colin apparently knew because *his* lips curved up and his tongue flicked against that spot behind her ear that she really, *really* loved when he teased. "Later," he said. "Later, I'll . . ."

And her jaw dropped open as he detailed every dirty thing he planned to do to her when they got back to their cabin.

Her pulse was pounding when he'd finished. Because, damn, his words were better than Abby's chapter sixteen.

"But first," he continued, "you're going to enjoy your sledding and gold panning, and then we're going to have a nice dinner."

"And a sauna?" she asked breathless.

"As long as you're naked and in my arms," he said, hand tightening on her waist.

Her lips tipped up even as her hand drifted down for a squeeze. "I think that can be arranged."

"I've DECIDED that I don't like gold panning," CeCe declared, falling back onto the bed.

Her arms ached, absolutely ached after an hour of shaking the pan from side to side and not finding anything more than silt, rocks, and mud.

"Not convinced you'll find your fortune in the river?"

"Even if I'd been dreaming of finding a huge nugget, *a la* Sutter's Mill, I think that this afternoon would prove I'd be crazy to continue with that fantasy."

Colin smiled as he plunked down next to her and gathered her in his arms. "What's Sutter's Mill?"

"Oh," Cecilia said, realizing that he probably wouldn't know much about U.S. history or what had sparked the California Gold Rush. "I got on a Netflix documentary kick awhile back and watched a ton of historical ones. This dude named James Marshall found gold in the 1800s and people came flocking West."

Colin kissed her forehead. "I like it when you say *dude*."

She chuckled. "I'm apparently a true Californian now. I say it to mean man or woman, senior or child, and as a curse, a plea, or an exclamation."

He nodded sagely. "You're a master of all things dude-related."

She smirked. "It's funny to hear you say *dude*."

"It's not that common of a word in Scotland."

CeCe rolled over in his embrace, settling atop of him with her chin resting on her folded arms. "But it has *so* many uses."

"Apparently." He stroked a finger down her cheek. "But the marvelous uses of dude aside, are you okay?"

"I think so." She paused, raising a finger when he started to open his mouth. "No. That's not entirely true. I *am* okay, but I feel almost . . . flayed open? I don't know how to describe it. Like I'm too vulnerable, and I keep waiting—" She bit off the rest of her sentence, knowing the words weren't entirely fair.

But even though they remained unsaid, Colin heard them anyway.

His eyes darkened. "You're waiting for me to hurt you again."

She hesitated.

He sighed and cupped the back of her neck, forcing her gaze to his. "No running. No pretending. I'm glad you're talking to me." He brushed a kiss over her forehead. "I'm so sorry you were hurt, sweetheart, and *I* won't hurt you."

Her heart squeezed. "But you can't promise that, Col. You can't predict the future. You can't wrap me in cotton to protect me from the world, and you can't realistically promise to not hurt me again. That's not real life." She stared into his blue eyes, seeing the truth dawn there. It was obviously something he didn't care to admit, but no one knew the future.

How could he promise to never hurt her?

It was unrealistic. Impossible.

People hurt each other all the time.

It's just that . . . she *really* wanted that promise from Colin, wanted for it to be the truth. That he would magically transform into that mythical hero, sweep her off her feet, and they would ride off into the sunset.

But myths were myths for a reason.

They were stories. Fantasies.

Fantasies that are grounded in reality, her heart argued. *That's where fairy tales come from. There's always a kernel of truth and reality within them.*

And great, now she was bickering with herself over the future of a relationship that would probably never be.

"I want to be the man you deserve," he whispered, and the torment in his expression made her heart ache.

"I want that, too," she whispered back. "So, so much."

Except she didn't believe in fairy tales.

She couldn't allow herself to.

Not any longer.

THE SUN WAS ALREADY low in the sky, but it did beautiful things to the silhouettes of the trees, made the snow glimmer with sparks of gold from the remaining rays of light.

Beautiful. Stark.

Alone.

Kind of like CeCe herself.

Except, she wasn't quite that any longer, was she?

Colin was there. They'd talked and she hadn't run and there were no more secrets and . . . he'd stayed.

Part of her brain couldn't believe it. Part of her heart was still in its protective casing.

She considered herself a generous person by nature, not one to hold grudges, someone who gave affection freely. After having the parents she'd had, she knew exactly how important compassion and understanding was.

But she was cautious.

Because she had given freely. Twice.

Her pencil began moving faster on the paper, remembering the whirlwind romance the first time—and the second—the big feelings, the way she'd loved Colin to the detriment of all else.

Trees flew onto the page, their shadows looking like disturbing skeletons sprawled onto the snow. The sun became an ominous orb. The sky a swirling fury.

Then she relaxed.

Because she wasn't that person anymore.

Yes, she was drawn to Colin.

But, no, she wasn't going to lose herself again.

She'd crawled, pulled herself through proverbial broken

glass to get where she was. Maybe she didn't have it all figured out. Maybe she wasn't ever going to be as kickass as Heather or Bec or as self-assured as Abby or even with a hidden steel rod of a spine like outwardly sweet Sera. But she didn't *have* to be any of those things.

CeCe just needed to be herself.

Or the self she'd figured out so far.

She knew she could survive a broken heart. She knew she could work and support herself. She knew that she was loveable—despite her parents' best efforts to prove the alternative.

That was enough.

Which meant she got to decide what her life would look like.

So . . . did she want Colin in her life?

Maybe it was stupid, but yes. Plus, she was allowed to be stupid because it was. Her. Freaking. Life.

And she wanted *this* Colin.

She wanted the man who'd spread out a waterproof blanket on the snow, along with snacks, her drawing supplies, and a pile of extra blankets, before waking her with slow, hot kisses that had threatened to melt her from the inside out. She wanted the sweet man who'd brought her to the blanket and who'd left her to her sketchbook that morning when she'd mentioned in passing the night before that she was itching to draw.

She wanted the man who was giving her space to do what made her happy, somehow knowing that she wouldn't be able to concentrate on drawing if he *was* there because she would feel guilty ignoring him while she drew. Instead, he'd stepped back and had gone to do something she had absolutely no interest in.

Ice fishing.

But it was more than that. Because she also wanted the adventurous man who suggested she continue ticking off all of her bucket list items for this resort, starting with horseback riding that afternoon. The one who'd apologized and owned up for his behavior, his mistakes, accepted her apology for her own.

She'd grown up.

And so had he.

"Which is why you haven't kicked his ass out of your cabin, Cecilia," she muttered, setting her pencil down and staring up at the sky. "Because no matter how much part of me wants to hate him for what he did, I know I'd have to hate myself, too. And I'm not that person anymore. I'm *not*."

Colin wasn't either.

Trust in that. But . . . don't *only* trust in that.

CeCe was going to trust in herself, too. In her ability to be strong and know her value, to stand up for herself and to leave if she wasn't being treated right. No more manipulations or punching bags.

Her life.

Her life.

Yes, she could do that.

Crunching footsteps drew her attention to the path that led to her cabin. Colin was making his way toward her, bundled up like crazy, but still giving major popsicle vibes.

She might have been outside for the morning, but the man had gone fishing.

On ice.

She shivered just thinking about it.

He stopped next to her, crouching down to brush a finger over her cheek, no doubt rosy from the cold. "Hey, sweetheart."

She shivered again, though she was uncertain if it was because he was touching her or because the finger that was on her skin was frosty.

"Hey, yourself." She cupped his cheek.

He winced. "Christ, woman," he said, hands coming up to

cup both of hers. "Your hands are like ice. Did you even use the blankets I gave you?"

Meanwhile, he'd been out on literal ice.

She grinned. "I'm wearing snow gear and was wrapped in a dozen blankets. I'm fine."

He shifted, wrapping a blanket around her shoulders, one she'd just shrugged off as she'd readied herself to move back inside because she was, in fact, cold. "You're a bloody icicle," he muttered, setting another heavy weight of blanket on top of her, hands rubbing briskly up and down her back.

She didn't move or complain for three reasons.

One, she was cold, and this was warming her up.

Two, *Colin* was cold, and this was warming *him* up.

Three—which was the most important reason—she liked being in his arms.

"I have a thought about how to warm me up," she said, interrupting his grumbling.

He froze.

She leaned back enough to shift in his embrace, enough to bring her hands to the back of his neck and tug him down on top of her. This time, he didn't complain about the temperature of her fingers, probably because she was determined to warm her . . . mouth.

On his.

Ha.

And with laughter on her lips, with hope in her heart, she leaned back onto the blanket and kissed Colin until she was warmed straight through.

"My thighs are so freaking sore," CeCe said on a groan. She flopped back onto the bed, phone pressed to her ear, as silence greeted her through the airwaves.

"Hmm," Heather said.

"Shut up," CeCe told her. "My legs are sore from riding."

"*Hmm.*"

One syllable from her friend. One syllable that spoke volumes.

CeCe rolled her eyes. "From *horseback* riding."

"Is that what the young kids call it nowadays?"

"Ha," CeCe said. "You're only a couple of years older than me. I don't think you can consider me young."

"Young at heart."

That made Cecilia burst out laughing. "Oh, Heather," she said, once she'd regained a semblance of control. "I know we don't talk about heavy stuff all too often, but I stopped being young the moment my parents disowned me."

A pause.

"I know about your parents, CeCe."

Any amusement faded. "What do you mean?"

"I—" A sigh. "You know we ran a background check when Jordan hired you to watch Hunter," she said quietly.

"Oh." CeCe sat up, feeling a little sick to her stomach. Heather had known? Jordan had known? That her parents didn't want her. That Colin had—

Heather's voice was gentle. "You don't own the monopoly on bad parents."

"Yeah—"

"You share it with Jordan and me, with Abby, with Sera, with Bec. Hell, it's practically the glue that binds our quintet." Heather's voice went earnest now. "We all have baggage. We've all spent a long time being a mess or dealing with the mess that is our family."

"I—"

"And further that, you proving that you could make a life for yourself, even after what happened to you, shows that you're fucking incredible, Cec. You can slay proverbial dragons. You can persist and keep going, and"—she heard the smile in Heather's tone—"you're somehow still nice."

"Heather—"

"No arguing," she said. "Accept the compliment and—"

"Will you just be quiet and let me get a word in edgewise?" CeCe snapped.

Silence.

She immediately felt guilty for snapping at her friend. Heather was just trying to be kind and was being a good friend, and CeCe had unleashed on her. "I'm sorry," she said. "I didn't mean—"

Then Heather began laughing.

"See?" she asked when she pulled herself together. "Nice." A beat. "But steel underneath."

CeCe was quiet for a moment. "I've never thought I had steel before." Heather sucked in a breath, probably to argue with her about the presence or absence of steel. Cecilia beat her to the punch. "But then I came on this trip. Then I realized I'm not weak. Then I realized that even though my strength is different than yours or Bec's, it's still there and rock-solid and important."

"Hmm."

CeCe snorted. "I see why Abby wants to punch you when you say that."

Heather laughed. "It's my superpower."

"Well, superpower or not," CeCe said, "it's annoying."

"My work here is done." She heard Heather clapping her hands together, as though she were dusting them off. "I should probably get off the line anyway. I'm getting on a plane in a few hours." A beat. "But CeCe?"

"Yeah?"

"I'm glad you went on the trip, glad you're using the time to recognize that steel inside."

She smiled, at ease. No, *loving* that one of her kickass friends thought she was tough.

Nice, but strong.

Yeah, CeCe would take that.

But she also had a little sliver of mischief, a piece of her personality that tempered all that nice, that made her just the tiniest bit wicked.

See? Her friends were rubbing off on her.

Which was why she said, "As for the riding . . . I *was* talking about horses earlier." She bit back a smile. "But I don't think it'll be *just* a horse for much longer."

Quiet, then, "You'd better not have picked up an interspecies kink."

"A man," CeCe said. "I'm seeing one." This time she couldn't hold back her grin and spoke through her smile. "And for the record, I'm planning on doing a lot of riding with him. *A lot.*"

Heather began sputtering.

CeCe laughed. "Bye, Heath."

She hung up, giggling, at the same moment Colin pushed through the door to the cabin, takeout bags in hand. He took one look at her face and dropped them on the counter, then closed the distance between them and kissed her until her pulse thundered in her veins, until her breath came in rapid gusts.

"Do I get to know what had you laughing?" he asked, pulling back, his breath hot on her lips, his fingers in her hair.

She shook her head. "Nope."

A wicked smile. "Should I keep trying to convince you to tell me?"

She lifted a brow. "Is that what you were doing?"

He nodded.

She wrapped her arms around his shoulders, tugged him closer. "Then yes," she murmured against his lips. "Keep convincing me."

Colin took her at her word.

And just for the record, the man could fucking kiss.

"I DON'T NEED you to do that," she muttered, wondering how she could have gone from having so much fun with Colin over the last couple of days to wanting to throttle him within an inch of his life.

"I'm trying to help you," he said. "I can set up an account for you, enough funds to cover your travel expenses."

This man.

This infuriating man.

They'd been arguing for the last ten minutes because she'd discovered that he had put his credit card on the room to replace hers.

A fact she wouldn't have found out at all if she hadn't gone to pick up their dinner and realized the last four digits of the card slip she was signing didn't match those from her card.

Probably why he'd said he would pick up the food after his shower.

Instead, she'd gone down, wanting to save him a trip, especially since he'd been practically waiting on her hand and foot.

Then the receipt.

Then the stubborn man in front of her when she'd come back to confront him.

Of course, he was just wearing a towel, and the white cotton hitched around his hips made it hard to hold on to her anger. But she was strong. She was steel. She would not get distracted by tiny beads of water dripping down a luscious chest she wanted to capture on her tongue.

Get it together, CeCe!

Blinking and forcing her gaze from his chest, she lifted her chin. "I changed it back to my card."

A cavalier shrug. "I'll change it back."

CeCe glanced up further, tilting her head back to study the ceiling as she struggled to keep a hold on her temper. "Colin," she gritted out, "it is very important for me to pay my own way. I worked hard to afford this trip, and while I was very touched that Abby and Jordan paid for my flight and gave me the voucher for this hotel, my intention is for the rest of the time and for all of my incidentals, to travel on the funds that I have worked hard for." She dropped her gaze, met the piercing blue of his. "I need to do this myself. *For* myself. Otherwise"—her voice gentled—"it won't mean as much."

He was a statue across from her, hands clenched into fists at his sides.

But by the time she got to the last sentence, his hands had relaxed, his jaw unclenched. His palm came up, cupped her cheek, and he sighed.

She braced herself, some small part of her expecting fury to accompany their argument.

Instead, she got, "I understand, sweetheart."

One half of his mouth curved. "I'm a stubborn bastard, I know that, and I want to take care of you. I have the means. But —" He ran his thumb over her bottom lip when she began to protest. "But," he said again, "I understand what it means to need to be strong enough to take care of yourself and to work hard for something and want to put it to good use."

Her breath shuddered out, and she nodded. "You'll leave the card then?"

A nod. "Aye."

She shivered, and he grinned, knowing it did something to her when he talked to her like he was her rugged highlander rather than a suave businessman. Which is probably why he pressed his advantage and said, "You'll let me pay half when I'm here?"

CeCe considered that. "That seems fair."

"And take care of you in other ways?"

This man. Stubborn as hell, and yet she really, really liked the perseverance, liked that he wanted to look out for her. "So long as you let me take care of you right back."

He grinned, brushed his lips over hers. "I'm getting the better deal."

"Who says?" she asked, raising on tiptoe and shifting closer. "Plus, I wouldn't turn down a private plane trip," she joked. "I know Heather raves about hers."

"Good thing I have one."

She shook her head. "Of course, you do."

He opened his mouth, probably to explain about the plane, but she found she didn't care about the plane, couldn't summon up any worry about making sure things were exactly equal. She'd brought up her concerns, and he'd listened. He'd backed up. Stopped and they'd worked together to find a compromise.

And that made her relax, made her able to enjoy this time with him, this process of building something new that wouldn't break either of them.

Also, her newfound wicked streak had made an appearance.

"Oops," she said, nudging his towel loose.

It hit the floor with a soft *floof*.

Colin made a strangled sound, but by then she was on her knees, was sucking him deep into his mouth.

He groaned, fingers weaving into her hair. "Cecilia—"

She put her tongue to good use, paired it with her hand. Maybe she'd taken a while to come into her own, maybe she'd been shy and a late bloomer. But she knew Colin, she knew how to touch him in ways that drove him crazy, and she knew that it turned her on beyond belief to have his cock in her mouth.

To give him pleasure gave her pleasure.

She pumped and sucked and licked and—

Found herself dropped onto the bed, her jeans torn off her legs, her boots hitting the floor, and her panties . . . well, they disappeared like so much smoke.

And then his mouth was on her.

CeCe forgot about giving him pleasure. She forgot about everything except the pleasure he was giving her.

His tongue on her clit, fingers circling her entrance, pumping inside. One warm hand slipping under her shirt to pinch her nipple between thumb and forefinger. "I—*oh*—like that, Colin. Just right—"

He pressed the flat of his tongue against her, curled his fingers, and—

She exploded, sparks bursting behind her eyes, moans pouring out of her lips.

It took a minute for her to be able to peel back her lids, another for her to push herself up on her elbows. She wrapped her fingers around the still hard length of him and began pumping.

"Sweet—"

"Not fair," she said lazily, although she tightened her grip when he tried to pull her hand off. "You interrupted me and my evil plans. I wanted to make you come."

His breath caught as she stroked him. "That's not—"

"I like you in my mouth," she murmured.

"You don't have—"

"And"—she leaned forward, traced her tongue over the head of his cock—"the best part of fighting is the mutual makeup orgasms."

"Mutual make—"

She took him deep, put her hands to good use, and—

He exploded.

"See?" she asked when they both could breathe again.

Colin cuddled her close, pressed a kiss to the top of her head. "I bow to your all-knowing greatness."

"Got it in one." CeCe snuggled in, yawned, and fell asleep with a smile still on her lips.

NINETEEN

Colin

HE STARED down at the woman who'd stolen his heart when he'd barely been a man and had never given it back. She was sleeping, making those soft noises in the back of her throat that he thought were the most adorable things he'd ever heard.

But the fact of the matter was that CeCe was it for him.

He'd almost ruined that, twice, but he had another chance, and there was no way he was going to waste that.

Her mouth had made him see actual stars, his orgasm burning a hot trail down his spine that he was almost surprised hadn't left him with third-degree burns. He'd been planning on just treating her to an orgasm. Instead, she'd surprised him, and then surprised him again after he'd had his mouth on her by taking him again, by sucking and stroking and—

Colin closed his eyes and breathed.

Patience. Slow, steady.

Not waking the woman he'd never stopped loving because his cock was in a constant stage of hardness around her.

He tugged her a little closer, rested his chin on the top of her head, and held on to this moment.

The rest would come.

Colin wasn't going to fuck things up for a third time.

———

SUCH A BLOOD-CURLING scream would usually send Colin running in, his proverbial sword at the ready.

Instead, he just glanced over and smiled.

CeCe was running around with two little boys, along with their mother, as they had a Boys vs Girls snowball contest.

Spoiler alert: the boys were winning.

Snow clung to the red strands of her hair, stuck to the back of her winter parka, clung to the waterproof pants she wore. Her cheeks were tinged with pink, the tip of her nose was red, and . . . she was happy.

The sight was a vice on his heart.

He'd nearly lost that forever.

"I think your CeCe is going to need a hot shower after this."

Colin blinked and turned to the man standing next to him. Sam, the father of the shrieking hooligans, who'd doused CeCe and their mom with snow, huge grins on their faces, laughter peppering the air.

The younger boy slipped and went down face first, accidentally knocking his mom down into the soft, fluffy stuff.

Colin chuckled. "After this, I think everyone is going to need a shower *and* a nap."

The mom, Lizzie, who CeCe had apparently befriended on the shuttle ride to the resort, grabbed the leg of the other boy, tugging him down and smushing a handful of snow into his chest.

Who then grabbed a handful himself and pelted CeCe right in the face, leaving her sputtering, green eyes wide.

Sam laughed. "Right. I think I need to get in there and referee."

"I'll come help—" His phone rang. "Sorry, I've got to take this. I'll be there in just a minute," he said after glancing at the screen and seeing it was the office. Since they were under strict instructions not to call, Colin knew this must be the equivalent of the building being on fire.

He stepped away, swiped a finger across the screen, and brought it up to his ear. "Hello?"

"Colin, we have a situation."

It was hard to hear Francine over the voices shouting in the background.

"What's the matter?" he asked. "What's all the yelling?"

"Your mother is here."

"*What?*"

His exclamation had CeCe looking up in concern, but he quickly slapped a smile on his face and shook his head. He'd deal with his mother. He'd just wanted a little more time, wanted to have a plan in place to make it clear to her that he would no longer tolerate her interference.

Apparently, there wasn't time for that.

He needed to diffuse this situation, make sure the business wasn't impacted, that his employees weren't dealing with the manipulation that was his mother. Okay then, he'd lay the groundwork of his boundaries.

And then he was calling his solicitor.

Because he'd wasted too much time. Because he'd let them hurt CeCe.

That wasn't happening again.

"Give her the phone," he said.

"You sure?" Francine muttered. "This is a lot. Even from her."

Heaven help him. "I'm sure," he said.

"Okay."

Colin listened to the rustling, to the loud, shrieking voice getting even louder. Then his mother's voice came on the line.

"Colin," she declared. "These . . . *people* will not tell me where you are."

As though his executive staff were peons of no value. Meanwhile, they ran the corporation that made it possible for him to step away, that paid for so many of the things his mother *had* to have.

Fuck.

He'd always known she was spoiled and selfish.

He'd . . . always been a bit of both, too.

But he wasn't that person anymore. He'd changed, and though what he'd done to CeCe, how he'd treated others still made him cringe, Colin knew he needed to be done with regrets and looking back. He wouldn't stop trying to make things right with the people he'd hurt, wouldn't stop showing CeCe how precious she was to him, but he also couldn't keep living life with the engine in reverse.

Push forward.

Devise tactics to handle his family.

Execute them properly.

He was planning on doing the same thing with his mother, his sister, and he was damned sure going to confront them, to make them own up to their piece in all of this.

He just needed the plan in place first.

"Well, you have me now," he said.

"I—" Her voice dropped to a hiss. "I'm part of this company, as well. I've made sacrifices and—"

"Have you?" he couldn't stop himself from interrupting.

"I—well. Yes, of course, I have."

"What sacrifices?" While Colin had been burying his father, while he was taking up the reins and ensuring that McGregor Enterprises didn't collapse in on itself, his mother had continued on as usual—burning through money, buying anything she wanted.

And Lana, his sister, was right in line behind her.

"What?" his mother asked.

"Exactly what sacrifices did you make, Mother?"

"I—well—I—" He could almost picture her chin lifting, her shoulders straightening as the imperiousness reentered her tone. "I don't owe anyone an explanation of my actions."

Colin wanted to snap back, to demand that explanation.

But . . . patience. Plans. Calm.

Slightly more centered, he tempered his voice and asked, "What did you need, Mother?"

She went off on a tangent about needing access to additional funds beyond what was in her account because there was a fashion designer in Edinburgh designing the "most exhilarating boots."

How footwear could be exhilarating was beyond him.

"How much?" he asked, interrupting the soliloquy. His gaze was on CeCe, his mind already shifted to the woman in front of him. The group was all doused with snow, their expressions filled with warmth and laughter.

Colin didn't want the ice on the phone.

He wanted CeCe. He wanted *that*. The joy, the fun, the laughter.

She was the sun, and he'd been cold for years.

His mother named a figure. A ridiculous figure for boots—unless they were made out of solid gold. "Fine," he said. "I'll reach out to my accountant." CeCe shrieked when one of the boys shoved a handful of snow down her jacket, and Colin had the distinct out of body experience of wondering why in the fuck he was standing there on the phone when all he wanted to do was be next to the woman he loved. "I have to go—"

"Where are you—?"

"Goodbye, Mother." He hung up, and cognizant that his mother would be persistent, especially when money was involved, he sent a text to his accountant.

Then he shut off his cell and shoved it into his pocket.

Scooping up some snow, he made his way over to the group, lifted his arm, readying to loft the ball—

"3, 2, 1. Now!"

CeCe jumped to her feet and launched a snowball at him. A snowball that was accompanied by four others, courtesy of Sam, Lizzie, and the boys.

Colin sputtered, dropping his own snow, and ran a hand over his face.

When he could see again, CeCe blew him a kiss.

He grinned . . . and tackled her to the ground.

And then, just because he could, he kissed her.

Then when she was breathing hard, when her eyes were glazed with pleasure, when there were plenty of '*ew!*'s from the boys . . .

He got her with a snowball of his own.

———

A LITTLE WHILE later they returned to the cabin, the tension from the conversation with his mother having dissipated along with the fading sunlight.

"Sauna?" he asked, closing the door behind them and rubbing his hands together. CeCe's nose and cheeks had turned pink in the cold and though she'd assured him repeatedly that she was fine, she was shivering.

"No," she said. "No sauna."

Then she unzipped her coat and dropped it to the floor.

"Wait," he said, rushing over to where she'd left her robe. "Put this on. You're freezing."

Her shirt followed her coat. Then her pants. She stood in front of him in a bra, panties, and socks. It might have been the sexiest thing he'd ever seen.

"I'm not cold," she said, walking toward him and yanking down the zipper on his own coat.

"You're trembling."

"Because I want you," she said. "So damned much."

"Sweet—"

CeCe shoved his coat off his shoulders, started tugging at his shirt. "Col. I *need* you."

"I—"

"Please," she said. "Please, don't deny me this."

Colin swept her up into his arms. "I was just going to say, I can take off my own clothes."

"Oh."

"Yes," he said. "*Oh.*" He set her on the bed and stared down at her for one long moment. That was all his ragged control could take. Then he reached behind her, unhooked her bra and exposed those gorgeous breasts. Her nipples were hard points, demanding his mouth.

He obliged, sucking one deeply while teasing the other with his free hand.

"Col—" She broke off as he switched sides.

"You're so fucking beautiful," he murmured, releasing her and kissing a path down her body. He stopped to tug off her panties, to nibble at one hip, to trace the path of freckles along her waist with his tongue. But those were mere distractions, side trips from what he really wanted.

Which was Cecilia's wet pussy pressed firmly against his mouth.

And it was *wet*. He could see it glistening, smell that musky scent even though he was still six inches from the motherland.

Her hips shifted, tilting slightly, legs spreading as he came closer.

"Mmm," he said. "You want my mouth, sweetheart?"

"Get your tongue inside me, Colin," she demanded, head dropping back to the pillow and her legs spreading further. "I need you."

He traced a finger through the damp heat, cock throbbing when she moaned.

Then he stopped delaying and put them both out of their misery.

One lick sent his arousal sky-high. It threatened to burn him to ash, to snap his last semblance of control. He was finally going to be able to make love to the woman who held his heart, and the only thing that was stopping him from thrusting deep and rutting like an animal was how strongly he wanted this to be about Cecilia. He needed to make it perfect for her. He needed her to see how perfect *they* could be together.

The next touch of his tongue shattered something within her.

She gripped his head, pressing it more firmly against her center and ground herself against his mouth.

"More tongue," she ordered, and who was he to deny her anything? "Oh fuck. *Yes.* God, Colin. Like that."

"Mmm," he murmured, loving the way the sound made her buck and grip his hair tighter. He firmed his tongue, found her clit and unleashed every trick he'd learned over the years.

"No," she said when he circled instead of flicking his tongue. "The other was be—*better*. Mmmm," she moaned.

Goddamn, but there was something unbelievably sexy about a woman knowing what she wanted in bed.

"Like that." Her breath caught. Her hips jerked and every muscle in her body went granite hard. "Oh, God. Yes. I'm so—mmm—I'm so close, Colin. Please—"

He slid a finger deep, curling it up and forward.

And she shattered.

Feeling her clench around his finger, her hands in his hair, her legs over his shoulders was fucking incredible.

But what was even better was her tugging his head up and kissing him before staring deep into his eyes. "Thank you." A whisper, but accompanied by a confident smirk that made him want to drop right back down between her thighs and repeat the process from the beginning.

She must have read the intent in his gaze because she grabbed his shoulders then reached behind her into that tote bag of hers.

Out came the string of condoms.

"Any interest in helping me use these?"

TWENTY

Cecilia

COLIN'S LIPS curving into a grin was just about the sexiest thing CeCe had ever witnessed.

Okay, fine. *That* was a lie. Even sexier was what happened next.

Namely, Colin making his clothes disappear with all the aplomb of a magician. There wasn't any room for embarrassment or insecurity. Hell, he'd had his mouth between her thighs mere minutes ago.

But this did feel a little different.

More intimate.

Especially when he hesitated by the side of the bed and just stared at her.

She propped herself up on one elbow, lifting her other hand up to rest on his stomach. "I like the way you look at me," she said quietly.

There was that grin again.

"I definitely like the look of you, lass."

"Not that again," she said, all drama as she flopped back

onto the mattress. "You'll transform me into a puddle of goo at this rate, I swear, McGregor."

"So long as you let me watch your diddies jiggle like that," he said, his use of Scottish slang for boobs making her crack up.

"Oh, my God." She slapped a hand over her mouth to contain her laughter. "You're terrible."

"And you have the most incredible breasts I've ever seen."

The intensity in his eyes made her breath catch, but she just tore a condom from the strip and waved it at him. "Enough pretty words. If you truly believe that, then prove it to me."

She didn't need to ask twice.

In a heartbeat, he was on top of her and kissing her with all the pent-up passion of a man on the edge. But, CeCe wasn't a passive participant.

Nope. She got in on the action.

She stroked and squeezed. She petted. She kissed and licked and nipped.

Until she could barely see straight from all the longing.

"Please, Col. I need you inside me now."

He didn't argue, just grabbed the little plastic square from near her head, tore it open, and rolled on the condom. He paused, knees between her open legs, cock two inches from where Cecilia needed it. But when she tried to cage him with her thighs and tug him down, he resisted. Instead of sliding home—where they both desperately wanted him to be—he stopped. Waited for her eyes to find his. Colin's warm palm cupped her face, the pad of his thumb stroking across her cheekbone. "You're sure? We don't have to do this now. We can take longer—" A shake of his head. "Keep doing other things." His eyes widened. "Or not do *anything*—"

Her heart swelled and she placed her fingers over his lips. "I'm sure."

Despite everything—the heat of him so close, her desire

raging low and hot and desperate, the past, the present—she *was* sure.

They'd been moving toward this for eight years now.

"I've dreamed about having you in an actual bed," he said, almost reverent as he nudged at her entrance. "About making up for . . . before. I thought often about making it better. Making it everything you wished it had been."

CeCe wrapped her arms around his shoulders and tugged him down so he was pressed tightly against her chest. "You're all I ever wished for, Col. You're all I've ever wanted."

He filled her in one stroke, gentle but insistent as he buried himself deep.

Tears blurred her vision.

Because it felt so damned right.

Because this was the piece she'd been missing. This wasn't a release, a mutual sprint toward orgasms.

This was . . . *Colin.*

His hips flexed, drawing back and out before pressing in, deeper and a little harder.

She moaned, and he repeated the movement. Then repeated it again. And again. Until the tears dried in her eyes and she was more focused on sensation than feelings.

Until she was groaning and screaming, demanding "More" and "Faster" and "Harder."

Until she was flying over the precipice and Colin was trailing her, growling her name as he tumbled, too.

Until her heartbeat slowed and reality returned.

He cradled her close for long moments, brushing back her bedraggled hair, pressing a kiss to her temple. Then, eventually, as though he were supremely reluctant to let her go for even a second, he slipped from the bed with a murmured, "Be right back."

His footsteps echoed down the hall to the bathroom. She

listened to the sounds of the taps turning on and then off before he returned with a washcloth. He cleaned her, returned the towel to the bathroom, and came back to bed.

There weren't any words exchanged as he pulled her into his embrace and tucked the covers over them.

CeCe didn't say anything as the sky lit up with green in a breath-stealing display, though the air caught in Colin's lungs as frequently as it did in hers.

She didn't speak until Colin's breath evened out and came in slow inhalations and exhalations.

Only when he was deeply asleep did she dare to murmur the thought that was circling her brain.

"What have I done?"

She had tumbled headlong into love with Colin McGregor.

For a third time.

Only time would tell if that would be the third biggest mistake of her life.

TWENTY-ONE

Colin

HE WATCHED CECILIA SLEEP, her chest rising and falling in slow, even breaths. The green in the sky had been short and breathtaking, though that hadn't stopped her from staying up too late, waiting and hoping for the northern lights to make an another appearance.

Of course, the hotel had installed an "aurora alarm" in the cabin, one that would be activated if the aurora borealis made an appearance.

Not that CeCe trusted that.

She'd said the first night as they'd lain bundled up in their robes, lying under the glass roof, "I've waited my whole life to see this. I'm not trusting it to technology."

Colin smiled at the memory.

She'd been like a kid on Christmas morning the first time the sky had lit that otherworldly green and it had made his heart catch, that little slice of the Cecilia of the past, the one who appreciated the beauty of the world. The one who'd stared endlessly over the cliffs near his home, studying the ocean and trying to commit the sounds of the waves breaking against the rocks to memory. It had reminded him of the girl who'd been captivated by the small details in a stained-glass window, the one who'd so appreciated the curls and different shades of color in his horse, Bowen's, mane that she'd spent long hours sketching every minute detail.

That had been the woman he'd fallen for.

The one with a zest for life, who'd been so freely giving with her love and affections. She hadn't been like the other women in his life, always calculating which power play would gain the most or throwing a temper tantrum when they didn't get their way.

Cecilia had been different.

And it had been their downfall.

"Fuck," he muttered under his breath, carefully sliding free of the mattress while being sure to keep CeCe covered with the blankets.

He had to make a call.

A long overdue call that would probably involve an apology.

Och. He hated apologies. Giving them, that was.

Quietly, he stuffed his feet into his boots and shrugged into his parka. He grabbed his phone from the side table before slipping through the front door.

Then he dialed a number he knew by heart. One he'd blocked six years before.

One he unblocked now.

The sun was just coming over the horizon, but it was already close to eight in the morning. Of course, Finland didn't get much sun this time of year, and it would already be setting by one in the afternoon, so there wouldn't be much of a chance to soak up its rays.

But none of this had anything to do with the call he needed to make.

Except to delay the inevitable.

"Fuck," he muttered again and pressed the green button on the screen.

Colin had a moment's regret when he realized it was two hours earlier in Scotland, but by then the phone was already ringing.

And ringing.

And ringing.

Then going to Ewan Campbell's voicemail.

"Well, fuck." He started to shove the phone back into his pocket, but it started vibrating, and one glance at the screen had his gut churning.

The arsehole was calling him back.

He glanced heavenward for one long moment before swiping his finger across the screen. This was what he wanted. Right?

Right.

He put the phone to his ear. "Aye?"

"You're a stubborn fuck, aren't ye?" Ewan said.

God that voice was his childhood, and the longing it set off in his heart was almost shocking. It wasn't a surprise that he'd missed the friend he'd grown up with, the one he'd gone off to Oxford with, but what *was* shocking was the depth of that emotion.

They'd shared so much, and Colin didn't realize until he'd heard Ewan's voice how empty he'd been the last few years.

"Aye," he agreed. "I think I might have misunderstood a few things."

"A *few*—" Ewan broke off then continued with a lowered voice. "A few things?" he whispered. "You misunderstood a whole hell of a lot, Colin."

"I'm sorry."

A pause, probably surprised, because he hadn't been the type of person to apologize outright for anything.

"Right." Another pause, longer this time. "You wouldn't let me or CeCe explain. Do you even remember what you did to her? What you said?"

Colin sighed. "She told me—"

"You've seen her?" he exploded. "After everything, she's let you near her?" There was a female voice in the background, a muffled protest. "Sorry, baby," Ewan said, and the sound of rustling filled the airwaves.

"Is this a bad time?" Colin asked.

"It's barely six in the morning," Ewan retorted. "That's never a good time. Especially when a couple is dealing with all the demands of a newborn."

Ewan had a kid?

"You're married?"

Ewan sighed. "Two years now. And my son is six weeks old."

"Fuck," Colin murmured.

"I know," Ewan agreed. "We're getting old. Growing up."

"I don't know if that idiom can be applied to me," he said. "Or not until recently, that is."

A pause, then, "You've seen Cecilia?"

"We're on holiday together." He kept the explanation as simple as possible.

"So, she trusts you?" Ewan bustled around in the background, turning on and off water as he filled a container. Probably for coffee. His friend had never been able to live without the caffeinated beverage.

"I don't know that she trusts me." Colin sighed and sank down onto the snowbank a few feet away from the cabin. "She's waiting for me to hurt her again."

"And you don't want to hurt her?"

His spine went ramrod stiff. "What the fuck?"

Ewan spoke over the sounds of coffee percolating in the background. "Hurting Cecilia seems to be a pattern for you. She's been happy and has a stable job. She's made friends."

"You've kept in touch with her." His voice sounded dead, even to his own ears.

"Yes, Col. She needed someone to look after her."

When you couldn't, was the portion of his sentence that he left unsaid.

Colin heard it anyway.

"I was in a fucked-up place. Not an excuse," he hurried to say when Ewan started to speak. "I made my first fuck up right, but I don't know how to fix the second one."

Silence.

Dammit. He dropped his head to his knees, a long tense quiet the only response to his words. At this point, he was ready to beg.

"Please, Ewan. I need you to tell me how to fix it."

A long breath hissed through the speakers of his phone. "There is no easy fix, you bloody idiot." A pause. "What you said to her was beyond cruel, and the only way you might have half a hope of truly repairing things is to give her time."

Time. *Fuck.* Why did it always come down to time?

TWENTY-TWO

Cecilia

COLIN WAS QUIET. *Too* quiet.

He'd come in a half hour before, his arms full of yummy-smelling baked goods from the restaurant near the lobby. He'd woken her with a gentle kiss and by waving a chocolate croissant under her nose.

But he'd been too quiet as he'd drunk his cup of coffee. All notes of teasing had disappeared, and it was making her uneasy.

"I'm going to take a shower," he announced, pushing back his chair in an abrupt motion that made her jump.

"Okay," she said, her heart picking up its pace.

Perhaps this was the moment he'd decide to get on with his life.

Without her.

Well then, so what? She wasn't that girl anymore. Her chin lifted, and she straightened her shoulders. If he wanted to go, then he could just let the door hit him on the ass—

He kissed her.

"I love you, Cecilia Thiele," he said softly, when they'd

broken for air. One brush of his thumb between her brows. She was probably frowning again. Then he strode down the hall, closing the bathroom door with a *click*.

But . . . had he just said *that*?

Why? How?

Blowing out a breath, she shook her head then ate some more of her chocolate croissant. Not in confusion exactly, but definitely in bewilderment.

"I love you," she murmured, touching her lips. "*He* loves me."

And he'd walked away again.

Well, that wasn't going to stop her. Not this time.

She put down the chocolate croissant—

Why did that make her giggle? But she could imagine a voice through a megaphone blaring, *"Put down the chocolate croissant and go attack your boyfriend—*was he her boyfriend at this point? Maybe? Did she want that? Also, maybe. But also, yes, she thought she did.

Anywho, she digressed.

Because Colin was in the shower, and her mind was still shouting, He needs a blow job, STAT!"

Cecilia didn't know what was wrong with him, what had happened overnight or earlier that morning, but he was off and unlike in the past, where she'd tiptoed around, afraid to rock the boat, she had already decided she wasn't going to be in a relationship like that again. So, she was taking a page out of her friends' books. She was going to bend less. She was going to clearly state what she needed in this relationship (yes, she'd decided that she wanted to explore what a relationship with Colin would look like), and she'd demand they talk things out.

No more secrets. No more sweeping things under the rug.

Because if they'd come together six years ago instead of

drifting about, caught up in their own traumas, things might have been different.

They might have still been together.

She stood and pushed back her chair.

Or maybe they wouldn't be together, maybe their marriage would have imploded in the end. But what CeCe was realizing with a growing certainty was that the past was the past and if she really did want to move forward with Colin in her life, then things between them were going to have to change.

Old patterns needed to break.

She stripped off her tank top, dropped her pajama pants to the floor, her underwear.

Naked, she pushed through the door to the bathroom.

Then froze.

Colin was fully dressed, sitting on the closed lid of the toilet, his head in his hands, the shower on full blast with steam filling the space in little gray, damp curls.

He glanced up at her intrusion, his jaw dropping open even as his eyes went scorching hot. His gaze dipped to her breasts, lower.

And while her stomach clenched in return—this man made absolutely every cell in her body stand up and take notice—her mind was more concerned.

She sank to her knees, feeling the damp air curling around her skin, placing her palms on his knees, the fabric of his jeans almost rough against her bare skin.

"What is it, baby?" she asked, slipping closer when he didn't touch her in return.

Nothing. Except his eyes closing and a deep breath expanding then collapsing his lungs.

CeCe reached up and put a hand on his cheek. "Colin? Has something happened?"

His eyes flashed open. "I spoke to Ewan."

Oh, fuck.

"Uh—"

"Why didn't you tell me?" he asked, agony in every line of his expression.

"That I still talk to him?" she asked when he nodded, keeping her tone gentle, considering that he'd thought she'd run off with Ewan six years before. "I didn't even think about it. Ewan has been good to me. He got me out of a bad situation, helped me get back to the States. But he's never been more than a big brother figure, checking in on me now and then." She sighed. "I wouldn't have let him be anything more, anyway. I wasn't capable of letting anyone in for a long time. But none of this makes any difference to what we're building now. Not with us looking forward instead of back. We should leave the past where it belongs."

Blue eyes full to the brim with pain. "I'm worried that I broke something we won't ever get back."

"You did," she said then hurried to add when he winced, "*We* did, Col. But we also don't want to go back, right? Isn't the whole point of this, of us being here, to build something better?"

Silence, then, "*I* should have been the one who was there for you."

Oh.

She understood now. He wasn't jealous of Ewan, rather her relationship with him was just one more reminder, one more regret, one more should-have-could-have-would-have. But before she could tell Colin that, his hands came up to grip her shoulders and though his tone was fierce, his touch was gentle. "Also, your logic is flawed. We are both holding on to anger and fear that is doing neither of us any favors, and if we can't let that go, we can't begin to build something better."

She paused and considered that. "What I feel for you isn't anger."

He stilled. "Then what is it that you feel?"

Love. But she was too scared to admit it.

"This," she said, stretching up to kiss him rather than confessing her feelings.

Colin allowed her lips to briefly collide with his before he pushed her back. *"That's* a distraction. We need—"

"No," she said. "What I need is for you to press your body to mine and hold me close. I need your kisses to show me what I mean to you, I need your touches to ground me in the here and now. Words are so easy, don't you see?" She dropped her head to his shoulder. "But actions are everything. Please, Col. Please . . . just give me everything."

He stood, helping her step into the shower before stripping off his clothes. "You already have it all," he said and kissed her.

Water sluiced over their skin, warm enough in actuality but almost freezing cold in comparison to the heat of his body. Nothing felt as good as him pressed flush against her, hard where she was soft, spicy where she smelled sweet. He didn't have the body of the gym rats she saw in Northern California, but his abs were hard and defined, and his pecs were squeezable to the nth degree.

So, she indulged, palming them, loving the way he groaned as she ran her nails over his nipples.

"I love you, sweetheart," he murmured, his breath hot near her temple, his lips kissing the delicate skin there. "I don't know how you can ever forgive me for what they did to you, for what I did and thought, for what I said."

"Don't—"

"I know. Actions." Colin's arms tightened around her. "But I *have* to say this. Yes, I was manipulated. Yes, they did a bang-up job of doing it. But, fuck, *you were mine.* I should—" He swallowed hard.

"I *am* yours, Colin McGregor." Her lips curved. "Always.

Even when I was fighting very hard against it, I could never deny this . . . this *thing* that ties us together. I knew it from the first time I saw your muddy boots on that hillside, stalking toward me, all brooding-hero-style"—she grinned up at him, relieved to see him smiling back—"and I know it in the man you are today. The one with agony in his eyes and regret in his voice. We both screwed up, but keeping hold of those old hurts will get us nowhere."

"I could just throttle them—"

"Baby." She rose on tiptoe, stared him in the eyes. "You know everything now. Can you let it go?"

He dropped his forehead to hers. "I'm so angry. We lost years because—"

"Because we couldn't find the strength in our relationship to talk it out." She brushed back a lock of his hair. "If we couldn't even talk through our second major hurdle—and I don't disagree it was a damned big one. But we didn't let it bring us closer. Instead, the deception imploded everything we had, and I think that means we were too young, and it wouldn't have worked out anyway."

"It damn well would have," he snapped.

She sighed, wrapping her arms around his neck. "I know I'm just riding this wave of crystal clarity that has come six years too late, but no, I don't think it would have. Sooner or later your family would have found a way to drive us apart."

Colin didn't say anything for a long moment, just held her tightly. But finally, he slowly exhaled and said, "You're right. I hate that you're right in this case, but . . . yes, I think they would have found a way."

"Words a woman dreams to hear," she deadpanned.

He released one hand from her back and used it to tip her chin up then brushed a kiss against her lips. "You didn't deserve any of the bad things that happened to you, and I will do my best to ensure every day from this one forward has something good in it."

"As long as that something good involves you," she said, closing her eyes and inhaling the clean, warm scent of him, "then I'm sold."

"And this *thing* between us?" he teased. "As long as it involves that?"

"Shut it, mister." She kissed his pec, flicked her tongue over one nipple, grinning when he moaned. "We can't all be Lotharios spouting perfect romantic sentiments." He opened his mouth, but she rose up to slant her mouth across his. "Now show me exactly how *romantic* you can be right here in this shower."

So, he did.

Twice.

And when they fell into bed later that afternoon, the sky already dark, the stars blinking cheerfully down on them, Cecilia fell asleep with a smile on her lips.

TWENTY-THREE

Cecilia

"I'M GOING to meet my friend Heather in Berlin next week," Cecilia said over dinner.

She and Colin had finally emerged from the cabin after doing little more than sleeping, having sex, and waiting for the night sky to light up with that otherworldly green of the aurora borealis for almost three days. But today she'd spent the morning sketching then several hours in the afternoon with Lizzie, enjoying the spa and getting in a little girl time while their various boys had whittled away the hours doing who knew what.

They'd also made plans to get together when they both returned to California, and CeCe was excited over the prospect of a new friend.

And then there were the magical auroras.

It still made her breath catch, the way those waves of emerald seemed to streak across the sky. She'd managed to see it twice more, bringing her total up to four incredible views.

And each time they appeared, the air still froze in her lungs and awe welled up in her heart.

But she was also going a little stir-crazy.

They'd panned for gold, done the dog sled thing, gone horseback riding, eaten at the restaurants, had food delivered. They'd read and talked. They'd fucked like rabbits.

Items were being checked off her bucket list left and right, but she missed the sun.

By the time they got up in the morning, the sun was already on its downward trek and when early afternoon rolled around, it was pitch black. The short days were messing with her mind, as was the isolation.

The staff at the resort were great at being unobtrusive, but she needed some people around. Needed to be able to walk down to the corner coffee shop and grab a pumpkin spice latte. She wanted to wear cozy sweaters and black leggings and infinity scarves, not parkas and snow boots.

She missed being home.

She missed Hunter and Carter and Jordan and Abby and Bec and Seraphina.

She missed her family.

But she had Colin, her heart reminded her, swelling like a balloon when he replied to her statement about meeting Heather with, "Do you want me to go with you? I know a great restaurant near . . ."

She squeezed his hand. "Don't you need to get back to work?"

He grinned. "I haven't taken a personal day in almost six years. Not since—" His smile faltered, but he pushed on. "Not since I buried my father."

"But—"

"It was the perfect way of hiding," he murmured, snagging a piece of meat off her plate. "But I'm done with throwing myself into work at the expense of a life that doesn't involve conference calls and emergency client meetings."

"Yeah?" she asked.

He captured her hand and kissed her fingers. "Plus, I think I can spare a few more days for the woman I love." Her heart skipped at the words. "My business partner, who also happens to be named Heather, will be in Berlin for a conference at the end of next week. It would be good to touch base with her before this project takes off."

"So, work even outside of work?" she teased.

His expression went guilty. "I—"

She stood up from her chair, crossed around the table, and plunked herself into his lap. "I'm teasing." A kiss to his cheek. "And you don't have to stealthily check your emails. I'm going to start doing some freelance design work for my friend Abby's company, so I might be chained to my laptop more than you."

"Why work on holiday?" he asked.

"So I can pay for my travels," she said. "And maybe visit a certain Scottish hunk on my way back to the States."

"Mmm, I like that idea," he murmured. "Though that would mean I'd let you out of my sight, and I'm not sure I can do that yet."

"Col." She touched his cheek, heart starting to pick up its pace. How could she have not considered the fact that they lived an ocean and a continent apart? How would they manage the distance? She couldn't drop everything and move to Scotland. Not again. "We're going to be okay, right? I mean, we'll manage the distance? I—I mean, I live in California—"

One hand rested on her hip and squeezed. "I'm rich, remember? I have a private jet that is always at the ready."

"But—"

"Plus, my new venture is based in California. It's why I was flying out of San Francisco in the first place."

"Yeah, about that," she said. "If this private jet is such a great perk, why were you on a normal flight with the rest of us cattle?"

"I'd loaned it to a friend." A shrug. "Next time, they're on their own." He grinned. "Especially since I'll be in California more than Scotland for the foreseeable future. This project is why I've been working so hard to consolidate the McGregor businesses, to make sure they're strong and healthy." He tilted his head down so his eyes met hers. "It was stifling, and I wanted to live my own life."

"But the dukedom? Don't you have to run it? You can't just leave it to flounder—"

"Being a duke isn't like one of your books. I might have the title, but it's all in a trust, and I have very good managers to make sure it's secure," he said, giving her a soft kiss before gently pushing her off his lap. "Now, eat your dinner. I've been planning to step back for a good long while from the non-technology ventures and turn it over to people I trust, people I've trained, who are long overdue to take up the reins."

There was something he wasn't saying, CeCe realized as she sat back in her seat and studied him. "It's not just that you were overwhelmed." She tapped a finger against her chin. "There's something else you're not saying."

He speared a piece of fish on his fork and announced like it was no big deal, "I was coming to find you."

"What?"

"I was going to start with your former coach and keep going with friends and family, talking to anyone and everyone until I found you." He smiled self-consciously. "Hell, I even considered trying to go viral. An I-messed-up-and-broke-the-woman-I-love's-heart post on Facebook or Instagram. I even set up an account on YouTube."

"You didn't!"

He pulled out his phone and showed her. "I did."

"Oh, my God." She dropped her head to the table. "I'm so glad you found me on that plane."

"Me, too," he murmured. "So, so much." And he took her hand, lacing his fingers through hers.

They finished their dinner in contented silence, their eyes passageways to all the overwhelming feelings in their hearts.

TWENTY-FOUR

Colin

"ARE you going to argue with me about this, too?" he grumbled.

Cecilia glanced around, taking in the tall stone buildings that lined either side of the street. They'd driven by an open-air market and several roadside cafes before arriving at the flat Joanne had reserved for them in the Bergmannkiez neighborhood of Berlin. Just down the street, treetops were visible, signaling a park.

"No," she murmured, and her face went soft. "It's perfect. Thank you."

"Good," he said. "Next time you see Joanne, you can thank her. She picked it out."

Cecilia huffed out a laugh. "You know, most men would take credit for making their woman happy."

Fuck if he didn't love the way she'd declared herself to be his woman.

Not that it wasn't true, but the sound of it coming off her lips was something special.

"So, a flat is okay but not a plane ride?"

"A *private* jet ride is fine *if* it's convenient for your business, but you redirected your plane so we could jaunt over to Berlin. That's a little different from a few days in a flat." Cecilia rolled her eyes then snagged the keys from his hand to let them into the building. "We could have just hopped on a plane."

"We *did* hop on a plane."

"*Your* plane." When she reached for her suitcase, he shooed her hand away, grabbing it and his bag. The rest of their luggage —their heavy snow gear—had been stored on the plane.

He tipped the driver, thanked him, and followed Cecilia inside the building. "What's the point of owning a plane if it's not at my beck and call?"

"What if the business needed it?" She shook her head and started climbing the stairs. "What if my little jaunt to Berlin did something to jeopardize your livelihood?"

Colin dropped the suitcases to the floor and ascended the few stairs between him and Cecilia. He snagged her hand, turning her to face him. "Is that what you're worried about? Each of the major divisions has their own plane, sweetheart. The one we flew on is *my* personal jet."

"I—" Her mouth opened and closed a few times, tempting him until he gave in to the urge to kiss it.

"Everything will be fine." He bent a little to meet her gaze. "Always the truth, remember? I promise, I won't hold anything back, but you have to as well." A kiss to her nose. "No brooding or throwing a fit when I want to give you a little treat."

"Brooding is a male characteristic," she said, testily. "And I'm not agreeing to being spoiled. If this"—she waved a hand around her—"is a *little* treat, then I'll eat my hat."

"*That* is a sexist comment." He grinned. "And I'll keep the spoiling in check if you promise to accept it graciously."

"Fine," she said, crossing her arms. "But that also goes in

reverse. If I want to buy you something, you'll accept it without grumbling."

"Deal." He snagged their suitcases and they climbed the rest of the stairs to the flat's door. Once inside, he set the bags inside the hall, shoved the keys on top of them, and scooped Cecilia up into his arms. She squealed as he kissed her, swallowing the happy sound, before using his foot to make sure the door was shut. Then he carried her down the hall, checking each of the rooms before finally finding one with a bed.

He tossed her on the mattress and followed her down. "Now, how about you accept something else without complaint?"

TWENTY-FIVE

Cecilia

SHE SMIRKED, staring up at the beautiful specimen of man above her for a moment, before wriggling to reach into her back pocket and retrieve a condom with all the flourish of a magician pulling a rabbit from his top hat.

"I think I can accept *something* without complaint," she said, pushing him to his back and tugging down the zipper of his jeans. "But first, it's my turn to give you a *little treat*."

Colin folded his arms behind his head, raised a brow. "Little?"

She snorted and tugged at the hem of his T-shirt, silently telling him to take it off. "Nice try," she told him, yanking off her own tee when he obliged. A shimmy later and her leggings were off.

He got a glimpse of what had been revealed and grinned.

"You like?" she asked, sliding her hands down over her breasts and teasing her fingertips under the band of her panties. The set was pale pink silk and very, *very* sheer. "My friends gave me a few parting gifts before I left California." She smirked. "Told me to use them on a hot European man." A tap of her finger to her chin. "Hmm. Where am I going to find one of those?"

"Behave." Colin reached up and tweaked one nipple through her bra, making her jump even as pleasure arrowed straight between her thighs.

She brushed her mouth over *his* nipple, flicked her tongue out. "I don't think you want me to behave." She bit down.

He hissed, fingers coming up to hold her head to him.

"Do you have more?" he asked hoarsely, when she slipped free and started tracing her tongue down.

She paused at the waistband of his boxer briefs. "Yes." CeCe pushed both his jeans and his underwear down, freeing his cock so she could suck it into her mouth.

"I'm going to kiss your friends," he groaned.

Releasing him with a soft *pop*, she glared up at him. "You'll save all your kisses for me."

"Of course." Colin nodded rapidly, arching his hips up, encouraging her back to her *little* treat.

"Good," she said with narrowed eyes before gliding his cock back between her lips, stroking her hand up and down its length until she found a rhythm that had him moaning and thrusting up, fingers clenching and unclenching in her hair, breaths coming in rapid gasps.

"Enough."

Suddenly, she found herself on her back, Colin pressing her down into the mattress. His eyes were wild, his hair askew, and his cock was hard and glistening against her stomach.

He didn't give her a second to process the gorgeousness of that image before his mouth was moving on her breasts, his fingers slipping between her thighs.

"Col—"

She broke off with a scream when he thrust his fingers inside of her.

He froze. "Too much?"

"No," she said, quickly. "Just give a woman a moment to catch her breath."

"No, I don't think I will." He was a flurry of action—sucking on her nipples, kissing his way down her stomach, flicking his tongue against her clit, stroking his fingers in and out, in and out.

Pleasure rose inside her with all the subtly of a tsunami approaching shore. One second, she was merely turned on. The next, she was catapulting up the mountainside, hurtling for the peak, screaming again as she plummeted down the other side.

There was a crinkle and then Colin was pushing inside, not giving her a second for her body to adjust to the rigid intrusion of him before he was pounding into her in a way that intensified the waves of pleasure still radiating through her, fanning the embers of her desire into flames that threatened to engulf her all over again.

"Col—" She broke off and groaned when he hit just the right spot. "Yes. *God.* Mmm."

"Look at me."

Her eyes flashed open and she met his, saw the need in their depths, the razor thin control he was grasping at, but what captivated her most was the love.

The last bit of fear, the piece she'd been holding back to keep safe. They both slipped away.

She was Colin's.

Forever.

"Give me everything," she whispered, her hands coming to his shoulders. "I'm not scared anymore, Col. Just . . . give me *everything.*"

He didn't hesitate, just leaned down to kiss her, his tongue thrusting in synchrony with his hips, taking them both over the cliff, driving them headfirst into pleasure on the other side.

And when he held her close afterward, their exhalations still jagged, both of their hearts beating a rapid tattoo, Colin murmured, "Everything is already yours, sweetheart."

SHE WAS drunk in a bar in Germany.

With a sexy Scot at her side.

Giggling, she leaned against his shoulder, loving when his arm wrapped around her.

They'd ordered schnitzel.

Actual schnitzel.

Another giggle had him gathering her closer. "You're well and truly gone, aren't ye?"

Heat bubbling in her stomach, pleasure coiling between her legs. "Mmm," she moaned softly, winding her arms around his waist and snuggling closer. "Talk to me some more in that sexy accent."

"You mean *my* voice?" he teased.

"Yeah," she said. "That, too."

Grinning at her silliness, he bent his head and began whispering all sorts of sexy Scottish sayings in her ear. And the man must have taken notes from her books because the things he said to her had her waving down the waiter and paying their bill.

Her turn, despite his glowering.

But the fact that he let her pay, paired with the gentle way he held her, and all the soft murmurings had ratcheted her desire to a fever pitch.

They pushed out the front door, headed down the stairs to street level, and began making their way to the rented apartment.

She'd just given into her urge to push him back against one of the brick walls and kiss Colin senseless when her phone rang.

She ignored it.

It rang again.

CeCe was just drunk enough to continue ignoring it.

Colin wasn't.

He pulled back and reached into her purse, grabbing her cell. "Answer it," he said. "Otherwise, you'll worry."

She would, too. And that he knew her well enough to understand that not answering the call would have kept her up when she finally sobered up enough to realize she'd ignored someone who was reaching out to her, unlocked another piece of her heart.

Time.

He was giving her all the time she needed.

Smiling, she cupped his cheek lightly and took the phone from him, sliding her finger across the screen and lifting it to her ear.

"Hello?"

"Cecilia?"

"Mom?" she whispered. Her fingers went limp. All hint of drunkenness left her system. The cell clattered to the ground, and she wavered.

Colin caught her around the waist with an arm and bent to grab the phone. He went to put it up to his ear, lips parting, but CeCe took a breath, finally centered herself enough to say, "No!"

Blue eyes on hers.

"I need to do this," she whispered.

A long look filled with pride, but also a battle. He was warring with himself. He wanted to take this over for her, and maybe she once would have wanted that, too.

She'd changed.

So had he.

Sucking in then releasing another breath, she took the cell phone from him. "Mom?" she asked, "are you still there?"

The voice was familiar and yet critically different.

"Yes, Cecilia," she said. "I'm here."

She sounded old. Frail. Stiff.

"How did you get my number?"

A pause then, "It's the same as before."

Oh. Yeah. That was true. She'd kept her number after she'd begun paying all her own bills. She just figured her parents had "lost it" since they'd never bothered to call.

THE MEMORIES of that time had the final tendrils of the cocktails she'd been drinking drift away, had her focusing on what was important. "Why are you calling?" she asked, forcing down the sharp ice pick of pain that thinking of her parents brought. Colin slid an arm around her waist and held her close as he propelled her forward on the sidewalk.

Taking care of her, but not taking over.

More defenses fell.

"Your father is ill."

CeCe waited, part of her expecting to be gripped by terror. Instead, she felt sympathy, *empathy* from the piece of her that didn't want anyone to be sick, anyone to suffer, but she also didn't want to drop her life and run home and play nurse by her father's bedside.

Maybe that made her a bad person.

Or maybe that made her someone who'd created her own family after her flesh and blood had cut her off, had abandoned her.

Abandoned a child. Because, for all intents and purposes, she'd been just a child.

All because she hadn't wanted to be molded into their form.

But her family—her *true* family—wouldn't abandon her. The one she'd created over the last few years. The one who'd brought her Jordan and Hunter, Heather and Abby, Sera and Bec. They would be there for her. They'd stuck by her side, and she knew they would continue to do so, even if she didn't do exactly what they wanted.

That was family.

Having each other's backs. Calling them on their bullshit, if necessary, but loving them even if they ignored advice or made a decision that wasn't the smartest.

Love. Loyalty. Support.

It was as simple as that, and the disparity between what she currently had, and what she had growing up, what was on the other end of the line was vast enough that Cecilia wasn't distraught.

Instead, she was resolute.

"I'm sorry he's ill," she said.

"Right." A clipped response. "So, when will you be home?"

"I *am* home," she said, and glanced up at Colin, felt warm when his pale blue eyes held hers, even despite the cool air.

"*What?*" her mother exclaimed. "Your father wants to see you. You will be on the next plane—"

Old patterns. More mortar for her foundation. For the decisions she'd made.

And maybe she should have unloaded, should have listed all the indiscretions that had hurt her over the years—cutting her off financially, not coming to her side when she was injured and recovering from surgery, slamming the door on her face when she'd returned home searching for some semblance of love and understanding.

But . . . the moment they'd slammed that door in her face, a door inside her heart had closed.

They were biologically related to her.

And that was the end of it.

"I'm sorry he's sick," she said, interrupting the tirade, "and I hope he'll be okay. You as well," she added when her mother began sputtering again. "But I've moved on with my life."

"You can't *move on*—we're family—"

"Funny story," she said, interrupting again, not caring it wasn't the least bit polite. "Once, I would have agreed with you." She closed her eyes, took one more breath. "Be well."

She hung up

Colin stopped their forward march, turned her in his arms, held her tight. "Do we need to fly back to the States?"

CeCe shook her head, another barrier falling at his use of *we*.

More proof they were building something together. More proof that the family she had created was stronger, more understanding, more supportive than the one she'd grown up with.

"No," she murmured. "We're flying forward, not flying backward." A pause, CeCe tilting her head, before starting to walk again. She wanted to be back in the apartment, alone with Colin—preferably with a *naked* Colin. "I'm not sure that makes sense, and now I'm sober, so I can't even blame it on that."

He snorted.

"But that part of my life is gone. It doesn't have any power over me now."

He stopped, tugged her tightly against his chest for one brief moment. "God, sweetheart," he said, cupping her cheeks. "You are so bloody amazing."

She started to shake her head, but then Colin kissed her.

Long enough that her pulse pounded. Long enough that her lungs burned for air.

He pulled back. "So *bloody* amazing," he said again.

Then he took her hand and they walked back to the apartment, the cool winter air a kiss on her cheeks, but the man next to her warm and solid and everything she had ever hoped for.

THEY WALKED up the stairs to the apartment the following afternoon, CeCe having slept late as she recovered from her overindulgence the night before. Colin had woken her at noon then had coaxed her into the shower and fresh clothes before plying her tentative stomach with several hangover cures—fried food and plenty of fresh air as they'd walked to a shopping area and hit several stores.

But it turned out that his cures were effective because she was feeling much better when they reached the top of the stairs and Colin opened the door for her.

"What do you want to do for din—" She glanced up and nearly jumped out of her skin, her shriek lodged in her throat.

There were people in the apartment.

Strangers.

And flowers. And a massage table.

And a rack of dresses.

Gaping, she glanced from the group of people, to the dresses and table, to Colin.

"Just a little treat," he murmured, nudging her forward before slipping back out into the hall, the door closing with a soft click.

"A *little* treat?" she asked, aghast.

"If this is a little treat," one of the women—a slender brunette with a hint of a German accent—said, "then I'm almost scared to see what a big one is."

"You know what it is," the other woman—also a brunette, but as curvy as her companion was thin—said, waggling her eyebrows. Her English was a little more accented, but perfect.

As was the innuendo.

"Ladies," the male of the group said, coming over and taking CeCe's arm. He sounded American and tugged her toward the massage table. "Give Cecilia a break. She's been thrown a curve-ball by the sexy Scot who hired us"—his pale brown eyes dropped to CeCe's—"to spoil you."

"He's *been* spoiling me," she argued, though Colin wasn't there to hear it.

But he had—taking her to several art galleries that day then shopping, during which he'd bought her a set of pencils that should be gold-plated for how expensive they were. She'd taken one look at the price after admiring them then had nearly skit-tered back in her haste to avoid accidentally breaking and buying.

And Colin had bought them anyway.

Stubborn man.

She smiled despite herself. Stubborn man that she loved.

Yeah, that was a *pitter-patter* in her heart, but it was also the truth. The man held a piece of her heart, had always had it, and the fact that he was so carefully cherishing it now undid her.

"Well, let us spoil you some more," the man said. "I'm Fredrick. This is Martine, and that lovely lady is Helene. She's your masseuse. I'm on hair. Martine is on makeup, and we're all opinionated as hell and will give you our thoughts on your dress."

He nudged her onto the edge of the table.

"Dress?" she asked.

"Yup." He glanced at his watch. "We've got two and a half hours to get you ready for dinner. Massage. Shower. Makeup. Hair. Dress." He clapped his hands. "We're your fairy godpeople."

Helene rolled her eyes and handed CeCe a headband to keep her hair off her forehead. "Come on fairy godperson. Let's let Cecilia change." Her gaze met CeCe's. "Clothes off. Face down under the sheet."

"Okay."

They disappeared down the hall and she looked around the room, stunned and touched and heart full. Then she stripped down.

Because she loved massages.

Because she'd never had one like this.

Because Colin had arranged it for her.

Smiling, she slipped off her clothes, pushed back her hair with the headband then slid between the sheets and got comfortable.

A few minutes later, Helene called out to her.

"I'm good," CeCe called back.

The other woman came in, and they spent a few minutes discussing what CeCe liked in massages and what she didn't and problem spots before Helene dimmed the lights.

Then gave Cecilia the best massage of her life.

An hour later, she blinked open deliriously relaxed eyes and slipped into the robe Helene left her. Frederick appeared, leading her down the hall and to the bathroom where he'd filled the tub.

"I thought you might like a soak better," he said, setting a couple of towels on the counter then fixing CeCe's headband so her hair would be safely above the water. "I'll knock on the door in a half hour when it's time to get out."

She nodded. "Thank you."

The door closed, and she hung up her robe. Then she was in the tub, warm water up to her neck. Someone had put a few roses in the water, rolled a towel into a pillow for her to rest her head on. She started to do just that, but then she noticed the book on the soap shelf.

Her heart thudded, and she dried her hands before reaching

for it.

A note was tucked between the cover and first page, and she knew even before she began reading that Colin had left it for her.

Her eyes hit the words, their meaning processed in her brain.

She giggled.

Chapter Twelve is good in this one, too.
—C

Fuck, he was good.

Smiling, she leaned back and started reading, and though it went against her normal rules of book engagement, CeCe began with Chapter Twelve.

She barely made it through, heart pounding, heat curling between her thighs when Frederick knocked on the door. She dried off and slipped back into the robe, carefully leaving the book on the counter. And then she let herself get swept up in the moment, in the pampering.

She'd never had her hair and makeup done.

Not even on her aborted wedding day.

She hadn't wanted to spend the money, so had done it herself. But that Colin had thought enough about what she might need to do to get ready for a nice dinner tonight, to have arranged Martine and Frederick and Helene, touched her beyond belief.

But even as her hair was curled and her eyes were lined, her cheeks contoured, and her body encased in silk and lace, she felt the streak of wicked make an appearance.

Which was why by the time the trio of her fairy godpeople had left, disappearing like smoke the moment Colin knocked on the door, that streak of wicked was in the forefront of her mind.

She pressed a kissed to his mouth, glad she'd forgone lipstick when he deepened it with a growl, tugging her tightly against him.

"You look beautiful," he said, voice husky when he released her.

"Thank you," she whispered. "For everything."

He brushed his knuckles over her cheek. "I love you."

Her lips parted, but before she could say anything, and she damned well was ready to say it in that moment, he kissed her again.

And she got back to wicked.

To chapter twelve.

When he pulled away to let her breathe, she slipped her hand into his pocket, leaving a little present behind.

Okay, a tiny scrap of lace.

Because the hero in the book had taken a souvenir home from the heroine after they'd gotten busy.

Because her wicked meant that she wanted Colin to have a souvenir to think of her all night.

"Wh—"

He reached into his pocket as she was slipping on her coat, as she moved casually to the door, and his growled out "*Cecilia*" made her desire bloom between her thighs.

"Chapter twelve," she said, smirking over her shoulder as she turned the knob.

Before she could open it, she found herself pinned against the wood, back against the door, front against all the hard, muscled, gloriousness of Colin. "Col—"

She didn't get any more out.

He simply . . . kissed her absolutely senseless.

And when he released her, holding her close as they made their way down to the car waiting below, CeCe knew that being a little wicked was absolutely worth it.

TWENTY-SIX

Colin

MUCH LATER THAT NIGHT, his phone buzzed, and he reached over to retrieve it from the nightstand.

Then grinned when he saw it was Ewan.

His friend had sent him a picture of his baby, a cute little bundle of unidentifiable gender, but held by a woman with love in her eyes.

The impact of that easy affection took Colin's breath away.

The reason I stopped drinking coffee for nine months.

Colin found out he was good at typing one-handed.

They're both beautiful. But . . . you gave up coffee?

Another buzz.

Yes, they are. And yes, I did. Without a second thought.

A beat before another message came through, before Colin had a chance to reply to the insanity of his friend having given up the beverage he'd all but built a shrine to in their younger days.

You know how you asked me how to make things right?

Yeah.

You make CeCe know she's yours. It's not just about giving up coffee because the woman you love can't stomach the smell. But rather that you will clear any hurdle for her, that you'll find ways to take care of each other and won't disappear at the first sign of trouble. It'll take time, especially given the past. But, you're a good man, and I know you can give that to her.

Colin sighed.

I'm not sure about the good man part, but I'm going to do my best to be one from now on.

The ". . ." of a message being typed, appeared and disappeared. Then Ewan's message came through.

Just love her.

That, Colin knew, was something he would spend the rest of his days doing.

"WHAT TIME ARE we meeting your friend?" Colin asked the next day, running a towel over his hair as Cecilia shaved her legs in the shower.

They'd slipped into a comfortable pattern of living together, sharing space and even a bathroom without a moment of awkwardness. Though . . . he grinned, thinking of CeCe's fantastic body covered in suds his hands had helped create in an effort to make sure she was *clean*. Co-ed showers certainly helped that along.

"At six-thirty for a pre-dinner drink and then maybe a meal if she can stay away from work that long," she said. "Heather's as much of a workaholic as you."

"Reformed," he said. "Your man is a *reformed* workaholic."

She peeked her head out of the shower curtain. "Who was up at three a.m. checking his emails."

"Fine. *Mostly* reformed." He kissed her, slipping a hand around the curtain to cup all his favorite curves.

"Mmm," she said, leaning into him before jumping back with a screech. "The plastic on the shower curtain is cold! Plus, as much as I like your mouth and hands and"—her eyes flicked down and she licked her lips, which pretty much turned his hard-on into blue balls—"*certain* other parts of your anatomy, I don't want to be late to meet Heather."

He rubbed his thumb across her nipple. "I can be quick."

"No, you can't," she said with a smile. "Which is why I love you."

Colin was grinning when she suddenly stiffened, and her face went serious. "What is it?"

She dropped the curtain. "Nothing. I just—I had better finish shaving."

Mentally repeating what she'd said gave him the insight he needed. He dropped his towel and slipped back inside the shower, carefully retrieving the razor from CeCe's hand before gathering her into his arms. "I love you, sweetheart. I've told you, nothing you say will change that."

She released a shuddering breath. "I know. It's silly, it's just last time I said that—"

He'd told her to go.

"You don't have to say it." He wiped a thumb below her eye, swiping away the moisture there. "I know how you feel. But things are different now, and if it accidentally slips out, I'm not going to run for the hills or be too drunk and angry and stupid to not recognize your words for the wonderful gift they are."

"*Colin.*" She thunked her head against his chest.

He wove his fingers into her hair, lightly tugged her back up. "What?" he asked, brushing back the water dripping down her forehead.

"You absolutely slay me with your words."

He waggled his eyebrows. "That's because I'm amazing."

She mock-scowled. "And modest, too." He grinned as he kissed her, feeling her answering smile against his lips. But then she gave him a little shove and tilted her head in the direction of the door. "Now, get out of here, I've got to finish showering so we can meet Heather."

"Okay," he said, giving her a sad puppy dog look.

"None of that," she declared, but her face was filled with amusement . . . that turned to heat when he trailed his hand down her front and slipped his fingers between her thighs.

"I'll leave," he said, giving her clit a teasing stroke before pulling away.

Her hand snaked out and caught his wrist, returning it to her heat. "Heather's always late anyway," she murmured. "She'll get caught up in emails and *ah . . .*"

The rest of her words were lost on a moan.

They were late getting to the bar, and even though he wanted to make a good impression on her friend, Colin found he didn't care.

Not when he was with CeCe.

Not when his heart was finally full.

TWENTY-SEVEN

Cecilia

"I DON'T HAVE to come with you," Colin said as they walked hand in hand down the street. "I can leave you to your friend and keep myself busy for a couple of hours."

She stopped and rose on tiptoe, giving him a heated kiss. The man was on fire, he'd made her come with his fingers then his mouth in the shower, all before he'd bent her over the vanity and given them each a release that had made them see stars.

"You don't *have* to hang out," she said, pulling back. "But I definitely want you there."

One side of his mouth tipped up. "Okay."

With just that, he took her hand again and they strode forward to the restaurant.

A simple request, a simple acquiescence.

Effortless.

He was just so easy to be with.

A happy sigh had him glancing down with a raised brow, and she just blurted it out, no fear this time. "I love you."

His hand twitched in hers. "I love *you*," he said and pressed a kiss to the spot behind her ear. "You're the other half of my heart," he murmured.

Her own heart twitched, and she bit her lip. "Romantic," she teased.

"Apparently." He tucked her against his side.

She tilted her head to glance up at him. "Besides me wanting to monopolize all your time, I'm sure Heather is dying for gossip to send to the ravenous crew at home after I told her I was seeing someone."

"Yeah?" He glanced up at a street sign and pointed ahead. "The restaurant should be just ahead." Then, though his tone stayed casual, she knew he was fishing. "What did you tell her about me?"

She smirked. "That you were trouble."

He huffed. "Women."

"Men." But she snuggled closer as she said it, loving the feel of his arm around her. "Thank you for chasing me down, Colin. I didn't think it was possible to feel this happy again."

The arm that was around her shoulders twitched, and he whispered, "I want to take you back to the flat and strip you naked all over again for saying that."

Cecilia turned her head to press a kiss to his biceps. "I want that, too. But first, food." They'd reached the restaurant and Colin held the door open for her. "Oh, look! There's Heather. I can't believe she beat us here."

CeCe waved, lacing her hand through his, and waded her way through the crowded space, feeling Colin falter for a moment before his steps picked up behind her. "Hi," she said when she'd reached the table and hugged Heather, who returned the gesture almost woodenly. CeCe pulled back. "You okay?"

But Heather wasn't looking at her. She was looking over

Cecilia's shoulder. "McGregor?" she asked. "I thought we weren't meeting until later in the week."

Cecilia glanced up at Colin. His face was as surprised as Heather's. "That was the plan," he said.

They both looked at her.

She glanced between them, smart enough to have put the pieces together, and lifted her hands, palms up. "Um. I guess our Heathers are the same?"

"Hmm," Heather said, shaking her head. "Well, sit down. How did this happen? Do I need a drink?"

"I've known Colin since I graduated from high school," Cecilia said, picking up a menu as Colin settled in next to her.

"What is it with all my employees fraternizing?" Heather grumbled.

Cecilia shook her head at the same time that Colin raised a brow. "Employee?" he asked incredulously.

"Fine," Heather said, holding up a hand. "Don't go all alpha male on me. *Business partner*. But first, there were Abby and Jordan, and now you"—she pointed at CeCe—"and McGregor. Abby just told me you accepted her offer, and you"—she continued her pointing streak, this time singling out Colin—"the ink on our contract is barely dry. How did this happen?"

"I love her," Colin said with a shrug. "Always have. Always will."

CeCe's heart gave a little *aw,* and Heather's mouth clamped shut at the words. "Damn," she said, glancing at CeCe. "You've got a live one."

"I know," Cecilia said, grinning.

"You also know the girls are going to want every *single* detail."

A sigh, but CeCe was secretly thrilled that Heather seemed to approve. "I know. I'm expecting it'll take several FaceTimes to satisfy everyone's curiosity."

"More than that." Heather chuckled and nodded her head at Colin. "Just *look* at him."

Col frowned, glancing down at himself in a confused way that made CeCe smile. "You're gorgeous," she murmured in his ear. "And perfect for me in every way."

He squeezed her thigh, murmured back, "What was that about *me* being a romantic?"

They stared at each other, eyes saying all the things their mouths couldn't in a crowded restaurant . . . at least until a *click* startled them out of their reverie.

"Sorry," Heather said. "I had to. You guys are just—" She shook her head, and Cecilia felt her phone ping on the group text she and the girls shared.

"Really?" She sighed. "There will be no end to it now."

Heather laughed. "Not for me." A grin. "I have to get off to a business meeting in a few anyway." She waved at the waitress. "This asshole from Savant Technologies is trying to undercut one of my deals. He thinks he's so flipping"—she rolled her eyes—"amazing and manly, and that just because he possesses a Y-chromosome, he knows how to run a company better than me. Idiot."

She asked the waitress for a drink then paused her diatribe as Colin and Cecilia ordered after quick glances at the menu. "I swear if he thinks that he can get the best of me, he's got another thing coming. *Ugh.* Sorry." She waved a hand and pivoted subjects so quickly that CeCe felt her head spin for a moment. But that was always the way with Heather. "I want to hear all about Finland. Was it amazing?"

"*So* amazing," Cecilia said, placing her palm over Colin's where it still rested on her thigh and then proceeding to chat away with Heather.

Aside from a few words here or there, Colin let them have their fun, and Cecilia did manage to shut up long enough about the aurora borealis to let him and Heather touch base on a few business details that had come up since he'd left San Francisco.

But then Heather was checking her phone and cursing, yanking her wallet from her purse.

They both waved her off, promising another get together in the near future and watching with wide eyes as she bustled out the door, fury in every line of her body. The crowd parted before her like the Red Sea, and a man scrambled to open the door, looking blindsided when Heather unleashed a smile in his direction.

"The man who's trying to undercut her is a bloody idiot," Colin said.

"Agreed." The door closed and CeCe turned back to *her* man, the one that was lifting her up instead of cutting her down. "So, your Heather is my Heather?" she asked.

His thumb came up, touching the corner of her mouth. "Apparently."

"Small world," she said.

"Very small." He smoothed back a lock of her hair, tucking it behind her ear. "But mine is so much bigger with you in it."

TWENTY-EIGHT

Colin

"I DON'T HAVE TO GO," he told Cecilia a few days later as they packed up the Berlin flat.

"No," she said. "It's important that you go and check in. I'll head to Paris for a couple of days and then if things work out, we can meet up there."

Paris. The City of Love.

He should be seeing it with CeCe.

"Promise you won't visit the Eiffel Tower without me?"

"Ah, Colin McGregor," she said, traipsing over to him and throwing her arms around his neck. "I keep forgetting that you're such a romantic."

He gently tugged her arms free and set her away from him. "*Woman.*"

"*Man.*"

"A promise, please."

She mock-glared, but her eyes were bright. "I'll wait on the Eiffel Tower, but I'm damned sure not waiting for you for croissants."

"I can deal with that."

Cecilia grumbled as she kissed him. "That's because you don't *like* croissants."

"Maybe," he said, deepening the kiss, sliding his tongue between her lips, loving the way she tasted so sweet, reveling in the heat of her mouth and the soft little sigh of pleasure that emerged when he was doing it exactly right.

They were both breathing hard by the time he broke away.

"I'm going to miss you," she said.

"I'll only be a plane ride away."

She laughed. "And you've got a private one at your disposal."

"True." He snagged her hand. "Come on. Let's get to that plane so we can drop you in Paris."

"I could have taken the train, you know."

Colin stroked a hand down her spine then gave her ass a smack. "I know. But—"

"You have a private plane. Blah, blah. I know." She stopped, abruptly turning around.

He froze. "You okay—"

Her arms wrapped around his waist and he struggled with the bags for a second before letting them fall to the floor. Who gave a damn about luggage when his woman had her arms around him?

After a few moments, she released him, heading for the door, explaining her actions with a casual, "I hadn't hugged you yet today. Oh." She paused; beautiful green eyes locked onto his. "I love you. Somehow more than yesterday, which should be impossible."

This woman was going to be the death of him.

But he was smiling as he followed her out of the flat and to the car parked below.

Damned if he didn't love her more every day, too.

COLIN DROPPED CeCe off in Paris with a driver to take her to the flat Joanne had reserved in the 6th Arrondissement then boarded his plane again and headed for Edinburgh.

He smiled at the memory of her pursed lips when he'd told her on the flight over to close the travel search site on her laptop because he had her accommodations covered. Those lush lips had puckered, her brows had pulled together, a fire starting in those green eyes, before she'd sighed, smiled, and given him a kiss.

"Thank you," she'd murmured.

"Have an extra croissant for me."

"I won't fit into my jeans if I keep that up."

He'd nuzzled her throat. "Then we'll buy you bigger ones."

She'd broken into giggles at that, and they'd spent the rest of the short flight chatting about all the things she wanted to see.

And now he'd left her in Paris, along with his heart.

"Damn," he muttered, knowing that he was turning into a sap. He needed to get his head in the game, to focus on business so he could get back to Cecilia.

He also needed to decide how to deal with the other thing.

The *thing* being . . . how he was going to ensure his mother and sister would never *ever* come between him and Cecilia again.

TWENTY-NINE

Cecilia

SHE WOKE WITH A GASP, hating that the old memories had arisen again now that Colin had flown home to Scotland.

During the day, it was easy to pretend everything was different and better, but without him, without the other half of her heart, old doubts began to creep in and make her uncertain. Was it inevitable that things would eventually go bad between them again? Would he misjudge her?

Would she end up all alone again?

Sighing, she glanced at the clock and saw that it was just before four in the morning. Too early.

But her friends should be available, Heather depending on which time zone she was in, of course.

CeCe opened the text chain and scrolled back up, past the Outlander gifs teasing her for finding her very own Jaime, past the pictures she'd sent of the croissant she'd devoured that morning and the very long line she'd waited in for admission to the Louvre. She kept going back until she tracked down Heather's travel plans.

And upon seeing that her friend had returned to San Francisco after brief stops in Rome and Madrid, Cecilia sent the S.O.S.

I need girl talk. I'm freaking out.

Immediately, texts began pouring through.

What's the matter? Abby.

How can I help? Seraphina.

Who do I have to kill? Bec.

Hang on, I'll videoconference us all in. Heather.

The screen of her laptop lit up and within a couple of seconds, each of her friends' faces was staring back at her from a different corner.

"It's the middle of the night in Paris," Abby said. "Why are you awake?"

Cecilia rubbed the aching space between her eyebrows. "I had a bad dream." Bec smirked, but CeCe waved her off. "Not like that. I dreamed about the day Colin and I . . . well"—she sighed, knowing that she was going to have to dish all. Their relationship status took *It's Complicated* to a whole new level—"We were supposed to get married."

"You're getting married?" Seraphina shrieked and clapped her hands together, her beautiful face shining brightly with joy. Sera *loved* happy endings. "That's amazing! That's—"

"Not what's happening," CeCe interrupted. "Colin and I were *supposed* to get married six years ago."

Sera clamped her mouth shut. Heather said, "Hmm."

Abby's eyes widened. But Bec said in typical rough and ready East Coast Bec fashion, "Well, fuck, the newest to our corrupted quintet of dirty old women has been holding out on us."

Already, Cecilia felt better. "I didn't expect to see him again. We . . . obviously, we didn't part on good terms. His family kind of conspired to break us up, and he believed them over me. I was hurt, so *damned* hurt, that I left and never looked back."

"And then what happened?" Abby was perched on the edge of her chair, clearly riveted.

All the girls were as she detailed the plane ride, the hotel in London, and Colin following her to Finland. Her life had all the drama required for their very own CeCe-centered romance novel.

"How's the sex?" Bec asked with a cackle.

Cecilia's cheeks went red-hot. But she answered anyway. "Incredible," she said, unable to hold back her sigh.

Seraphina giggled. "I'll take what she's having."

Heather spoke for the first time. "So, it seems like everything is going good and that you worked out a lot of your issues. Plus, he couldn't keep his eyes—or hands—off you at dinner the other day. What's going on now that has you doubting him?"

"I'm not doubting necessarily . . ." she prevaricated.

"Try that line on a different group of horny old women," Bec said.

"I resent the term *old*," Abby said.

Bec waggled her brows. "But not horny?"

"Clearly not." Abby pointed at her slightly rounded belly.

"Ladies," Heather interjected. "I know you think you're amusing, but CeCe needs to answer the question."

She flopped back onto the bed, staring up at the gorgeous antique ceiling. It was coffered and the swirling white wood-work was so gorgeous that she physically ached for her sketchbook. "I'm not doubting his intentions." She groaned. "I'm just doubting our . . . *I don't know*, our staying power, I guess. I mean, he's been sweet before, and now he's not here, and what if it all goes to shit again? I can't—I don't know how—"

"You miss him," Sera said.

"Yes," she wailed. "And now he's back in Scotland, and what if his family gets their claws into him again?"

"Then he's a fucking idiot," Heather said bluntly.

"And we cut off his balls with rusty scissors," Bec added.

CeCe sat up, nose wrinkling. "Why rusty?" she asked.

A shrug. "Because that's worse."

"Okay," she said, not able to disagree with that logic.

"Why not just fly to Scotland?" Abby asked. "If you're not going to enjoy your solo time in Paris, you might as well visit him and spend some more time together."

"And hot sex," Bec said. "She needs more of that."

Seraphina nodded. "I agree. This will give you both a chance to flush away those bad memories and move forward. It's not like he can avoid his family forever."

"I bet he wishes he could," Heather grumbled. "Family is a giant pain in the ass—"

"Hey!" Abby said with a glare.

"Present company excluded," Heather said, smirking. "But his business is also based in Scotland, so he'll need to go back regularly. If you can't get over that . . ."

Heather didn't finish the rest of the sentence, but Cecilia heard it anyway. If she didn't get over her discomfort with Scotland—going there, him returning home, his family—they would be stuck in this same painful cycle forever.

It was better to rip off the Band-Aid.

"I guess I'm going to Scotland."

"You pack, and I'll get Jordan's assistant to book you on a flight," Abby said. "I'll text you the details."

"What's it with billionaires and assistants?" CeCe muttered.

Abby just grinned. "You know you love it."

She rolled her eyes. "Fine. I do." A glance at her friends. "You guys are amazing. Thank you."

"Pish," Bec said.

"Love you!" Seraphina called.

Carter ran onto the screen and waved at CeCe. "We love you, too," Abby called over his chattering.

"Remember," Heather said. "Our demons only drag us down if we give them the power to do so."

Cecilia's breath caught; she opened her mouth to—

Bec beat her to it. "Fuck, that was deep."

"Language!" Abby chided.

Sera just smiled as Heather shook her head, hand reaching forward in her little corner of the screen. "Talk soon." CeCe's laptop screen went black.

"I guess I'm doing this," she said and headed for the bathroom to shower.

Scotland, here I come.

THIRTY

Colin

HIS PHONE RANG, and a grin broke out on his face. "Sorry, gentlemen," he told the group of investors sitting at the table with him. "I've got to take this, but Francine has the matter well in hand. You can direct any further concerns to her."

Hopefully, him saying the actual words would prevent Colin from having to make this type of trip again.

Tetchy investors not wanting to work with his female CFO.

Bloody idiots.

But if this impromptu meeting didn't work, if they continued to circumvent Francine, then they could take their money elsewhere. McGregor Enterprises wasn't desperate for investment, and Francine was the best person for the job—male, female, or otherwise.

"Sweetheart," he said after he'd swiped a finger across the screen and made sure the conference room door was closed behind him.

"I-is this a bad time?"

Colin frowned as he strode into his office. "No." He wanted

to find the words to put her completely at ease but knew there wasn't one perfect thing he could say. That, unfortunately, rebuilding the trust she had in him would take time. "Cecilia, I'm here for you," he said. "Whenever you need."

Her breath rattled through the speakers. "Well, I'm glad you said that because I . . . uh . . .I—"

"Sweetheart, what is it?"

"I kind of flew to Scotland to surprise you," she blurted. "But I didn't think about where you would be. I don't where your office is, and I'm at the airport and—"

He cut her off. "Cecilia."

"Yes?" she asked, her voice small.

"I'm sending a car to pick you up. Neil was already dropping off someone for a flight to Dubai, so he can get to you sooner than I could. What terminal are you in?"

She told him, and he put her on speaker to fire off a text.

"Okay. He'll be there in ten minutes. Can you go wait on the curb for him?"

He sensed her nodding, heard the sounds change as she began to move. "I'm here."

"Good," he said then hesitated before asking anyway. "What's the matter?"

"I—uh . . . I'm sorry. It was stupid to come here."

Colin started packing up his briefcase. "Did I somehow give you the impression that I don't want you here? I just wish I could have had someone waiting. I don't like you standing out in the cold."

"I should have told you."

"Cecilia," he said again. "I'd already called to have the jet readied for takeoff to Paris in a couple of hours."

"Oh," she said softly.

Colin decided to lay all his cards on the table. It was the only way they'd be able to keep building something healthy between them. "The truth is, I was missing you desperately. I hate being here when you're not." He smiled at his receptionist as he left. "I'm so, *so* glad you're here."

She released a shuddering breath. "Really?"

"Really," he said and too impatient to wait for the elevator, he pounded down the stairs to where his driver waited. "Now, Neil is going to take you to my flat. I'll be there and waiting by the time you arrive from the airport."

"Okay." Her next word was light. "Naked?"

He laughed, a full bark that made his driver, Mick, send a shocked glance in his direction. Colin didn't think he'd ever smiled at the other man, let alone laughed. He wasn't an asshole, but he hadn't had much to laugh about over the last few years.

"Your flat?" Mick asked, opening the back door.

Colin nodded. "Thanks." To CeCe he said, "Stay on the line with me until Neil gets there."

"Okay," she said then, "Did you really miss me?"

"Sweetheart." He smirked. "Don't ask stupid questions."

"Hey!"

"Is for horses," he said, stealing one of her lines.

"Oh, my God," she muttered. "I can't believe you remember that."

"A certain redhead might have taught me a few American idioms."

She snorted.

"And, yes, I really did miss you," he said. "Did you have enough croissants?"

CeCe huffed out a laugh. "Never! Oh, I think he's here. Dark hair, green eyes, and glasses. A Mark Wahlberg lookalike?"

"Not sure who *that* is," he replied. "But Neil is supposed to show you his identification."

"*Hi, ma'am,*" Colin heard. "*Can I take your bag?*"

"He flashed a fancy badge," Cecilia whispered, and Colin relaxed.

"Good. See you in thirty minutes, sweetheart."

"Can't wait," she murmured before clicking off.

And Colin knew he had the biggest, dopiest smile ever on his face, but he found he didn't give a damn.

Then his phone rang again.

"Sweetheart," he began. "It's only—"

His mother's voice was shrill as it screamed through the speaker. "Colin Douglas McGregor, what *have* you done?"

Fury filled his every cell.

After everything, every-*bloody*-thing, his mother and sister had done, *this* was her first reaction to his request?

Fucking hell.

There would be no more playing nice.

His lips twisted into a smile that must have been more feral than kind. "Mother," he said. "So good to hear from you. Cecilia and I will be over for brunch tomorrow." A pause. "That should give you plenty of time to pack."

"You—"

"Great," he interrupted. "I'll see you then."

Colin hung up the phone, silencing it when she called back, and then several more times when she continued trying to get through. Finally, when it seemed as though she'd taken the hint, he shoved his cell into his pocket, pushed her from his mind, and asked Mick to stop the car for a moment. He cleaned out a bakery of their croissants—not French, but they did look damned good—and then picked up a bouquet of yellow daffodils.

See? He'd listened *and* learned.

Now was his chance to prove that to the woman he loved.

THIRTY-ONE

Cecilia

SHE SMILED and stroked a finger down one of the yellow petals of the daffodils Colin had surprised her with. "Thank you for the flowers."

He pressed a kiss to her bare shoulder. "I didn't think you'd even noticed them, given the way you launched yourself at me when I opened the door."

"*You* grabbed *me*."

A chuckle against her spine then a sharp nip at her cheek . . . the lower one.

"Colin!"

"Mmm." His tongue darted out to soothe the sting. "I really liked *your* surprise."

She played innocent. "Me flying in?"

"Not that one."

"The bottle of wine?"

He kissed over the rounded curve of her butt, drifting slowly down and inward. "Nope."

"The cheese—"

He licked, and she broke off on a gasp.

"Uh-uh." Another lick. Calloused fingers spreading her legs a little wider.

"My lingerie?"

"Mmm-hmm." He pressed an open-mouth kiss to her clit and she jumped, then sighed as his fingers joined the party, showing just how much he'd enjoyed the sheer lacy garter belt and bra set.

It had been another gift from the girls, and it matched her eyes perfectly. It also enhanced certain other parts of her anatomy.

She'd sent them a mental thank you when Colin's eyes had nearly popped out of his head.

Colin licked her again and any thoughts of lingerie faded from her mind. No, *all* thoughts faded. Her brain was hazed with the desire for more. For faster. For *again, right there.*

"Oh God, please do that again," she moaned when his tongue executed some twisting movement that nearly toppled her over the edge.

And he did, but thank everything that was holy, he did it again. And again. And then once more. Until she was hurtled into space, and pleasure coursed through every cell of her body.

"You're really fucking good at that," she said, once she'd managed to regain one half of a wit.

He grinned, like a cat that had gotten into the cream.

And he had *gotten the cream,* she thought with an inner cackle that would have made Bec proud.

"Give me five minutes," she said, "and I'll be smiling that way at you."

Colin crawled up the bed, hauling her into his arms. "I didn't do it because I wanted something in return."

"I know." She sighed and cuddled closer, still limp and satiated but knowing that she needed to broach this subject sooner rather than later. Cecilia really wanted the black cloud that was hanging over them gone forever. "But I like doing it and"—she prepped herself for the rapid left turn in conversation she was about to throw at him—"Colin, I think we need to go see your family."

He shuddered. "Those two topics should never be spoken about in the same sentence."

"I—" She shook her head, smacked him across the chest. "You know that's not what I meant."

A brush of his fingers across her cheek. "I know. And funny that you should bring it up, but I told my mother we were coming for brunch tomorrow."

"*What?*"

"Right after I sent her an official letter from my solicitor demanding that she and Lana vacate the estate within thirty days."

"But—"

"They're not going to be destitute. I've bought them a house." A shrug. "It's on the other side of the country, but it's opulent, and they'll still receive their portions of the company's profits." He stopped and stared down at her. "I can't look at them. I can't pretend to love them after all they've done to you. It wasn't right."

"They're your family though."

"Real family doesn't act that way."

Cecilia thought about her own parents, about all they'd done—and *hadn't* done—and knew he was right. Jordan and Hunter, Abby, Heather, and the girls were more family than her own blood.

"You're right."

"Of course, I am." He smirked but cupped her cheek with gentle fingers. "You don't have to go if you don't want to."

"Oh no. I definitely want to clear the air. Now, about that

cocky smile you were sending my way a few minutes ago," she said, her hand snaking down his stomach.

Colin's groan was enough to rid her of any doubt.

This was right.

He'd talked to her. He was going to have her back with his family.

He loved her.

CeCe sighed contentedly. This time they were going to make it.

───────

COLIN OPENED her car door then laced his fingers through hers as they walked up the drive. The McGregor Estate, informally called Rock Hill, loomed large and gloomily overhead.

She used to love those spires and the way the windows curved at their top corners.

Today it looked as bleak as she felt inside.

The last time she'd seen this place—

So. Not. Going. There.

Colin released her hand but snaked an arm around her waist, tugging her flush against his side. "I'm here."

CeCe melted. This man . . . he was it.

The front door opened before they could knock, and CeCe was surprised to see Joanne.

"Oh, look at you!" she said, running toward them to grab Cecilia's shoulders. "You're as pretty as ever." Then she hugged her tight, whispering in her ear, "Did my Col make things right between you?"

"Yes." Her lips twitched as Joanie pulled back. "Now I know how he heard about the daffodils."

Joanne winked before turning to hug Colin.

"Your mother and sister are in the study and . . . Olivia is there, too."

Cecilia's heart clenched, she'd only met Olivia a handful of times, and most of those had only been in passing because Lana, Colin's sister, and Olivia were friends. Olivia Stewart was beautiful and had seemed sweet, at least until Ewan had implicated her in her and Colin's breakup.

Colin just nodded grimly at Joanne's words, pulled CeCe close again, and led them inside. "Can you send a tray into the study?" he asked. "We haven't eaten yet."

They'd been too busy christening his shower.

And then his kitchen counter.

And the front door.

Those memories shored up her spine. She could totally do this.

But that was before they actually walked into the study, because the trifecta of beautiful and cold women standing before her was beyond intimidating.

No one spoke as Colin settled her in a chair and then sat on the arm of it.

He placed a hand on her shoulder when she opened her mouth to break the awkward silence. *Wait*, he seemed to be telling her.

She gave him a small nod.

Bridget, his mother, was the one to cave. "How could you do this to us?" she wailed. "This stupid American bitch has you on tenterhooks again, and you'll just throw over your family for *her?*"

Olivia winced, but Lana inclined her head, encouraging her mother along.

"First. Don't ever talk about Cecilia like that again." Colin's tone was frigid, and she shivered from the force of it. "Second, is that *really* all you have to say for yourself?"

"All *I* have to say?" Bridget pointed a bony finger at CeCe. "*She—*"

"Actually," Olivia interrupted, looking extremely frightened but determined all the same. "I *do* have something to say." She stood and crossed over to where Cecilia sat. "I'm so sorry. I was" —her eyes were glassy—"well, it doesn't matter what I was. It was horrible and wrong, and you need to know that I forged—"

"Shut up!" Lana snapped. "You're supposed to be helping, not—"

Colin leveled a glare at his sister that had her paling and clamping her mouth shut. "Go on," he said, his tone so soft it was almost deadly.

Olivia took a deep breath, releasing it before the words poured out. "I took Cecilia's journal and helped Lana set up an account to make it look like she was stealing. Then I sent Ewan to the church, following him with my camera so I could take pictures, making it look like she'd run off with him." She bit her lip. "This is all my fault."

"Why?" CeCe asked. "Why would you do that?"

Olivia's eyes dropped to the carpet. "I wanted to marry him."

"Oh," CeCe said dumbly. It was an obvious reason, she supposed, just not one that she'd ever considered. Her eyes lifted first to Bridget then to Lana. "You wanted that, too."

Not a question.

Lana still answered it as though it were one. "Obviously."

"I—" CeCe shook her head. "Wow."

"I'm so sorry," Olivia said. "I know it was wrong and—" She reached out a hand, as though to touch Colin's arm, but the look he gave her had that palm freezing midair and returning to her side. "I was a jealous coward," she told them. "No. *Worse* because I didn't confess my part in it until now." A tear slipped from the corner of her eye. "I robbed you of y-years. I'm so sorry."

What could CeCe say? *It's okay?* But it wasn't.

Instead, she settled on, "Thank you for telling us."

Olivia dropped to her knees in front of them. "Colin. I'm so sorry. Please, forgive me."

His gaze flicked in her direction then away, fury in the clenched line of his jaw. "No."

Olivia wilted, and CeCe found she didn't have it in her to make the other woman feel worse. Not when she was already so torn up. "We've all made a lot of mistakes." She patted Olivia's hand. "Should we try to move forward now?"

A tearful nod. "I'd like that."

"Good."

Colin shot a dismissive glance in Olivia's direction. "Anything else?"

She shook her head.

"Good. Leave."

Bridget and Lana gasped. "You can't talk to her like that," Lana said, but Olivia just sent them one more apologetic look before leaving the room.

"What have you got to say for yourselves?" he lobbed the question to the room.

"You can't honestly believe her," Bridget attempted. "They must be working together—"

Colin stood, hands fisted at his sides. "Shut. Up."

"You know what I don't get," Cecilia said, touching Colin's back in an effort to calm him. Then pushed past her discomfort to ask the next question. She needed to know the answer. "Why go through the effort? Why befriend me? Why make me feel like part of the family?"

Lana rolled her eyes, but Bridget's were as cold as those

nights in Finland. "You took him from me," she hissed. "You were never supposed to come back."

Cecilia snagged Colin's hand when he would have strode over to them.

"I guess fate had different plans because I never did expect to be back here again." She tangled her fingers with his. "But I'm so glad I am, because everything you did to tear us apart has actually made us stronger in the end."

"You can't have him!" Bridget shrieked. "He's mine. The money is mine—" She broke off, panic on her face for one brief second before her tone took such a dramatic turn—bitchy to sweet—that CeCe could see how easily they'd been manipulated. She'd seen the sharp side of Bridget many times during their engagement, but it had been so quickly covered up by softness, by supposed caring, that it had been far simpler for her brain to chalk it up to *her* misunderstanding, rather than because Colin's mom was a complete and utter asshole.

"Colin, dear, I love you," Bridget began, so sickly sugary now that CeCe understood the truth beneath those words that it made her teeth ache. "I need you, especially with your father gone. I'm so lonely—"

"Enough," Colin said, sitting back down on the arm of the chair. "Let me make this easy on you. Your *money* is safe, but the only way you'll see another pound is if you get the hell out of this house and *never* come back."

"You can't cut us out of the business's profits," Lana said, chiming in at precisely the wrong time. Especially when she wasn't tempering her tone with any of the falseness her mother had adopted. Her expression was predatory and calculating.

Colin's smile in response was wolfish. "Oh, but I can."

"*You wouldn't.*"

He shrugged as if to say, *Wouldn't I?* and the smug expression on Lana's face slipped.

"Now, you can enjoy your fat inheritance far, far away from here in the home I bought for you or buy one in another bloody country for all I care, but neither of you will ever be welcome in this house again."

"But—"

Joanne bustled in, a tray heaped with food held aloft. "Hungry, dears?"

"No," Lana and Bridget snapped.

"Great," Colin said, tilting his head toward the open door. "Then you can finish packing your things."

THIRTY-TWO

Colin

A FEW WEEKS LATER, Colin rode out from the stables atop his black gelding, Bowen, heading in the direction of the outer edge of his property. He knew that CeCe had probably ended up there, even though his groom had told him she'd started that morning in the opposite direction.

His woman was a creature of habit, enjoying a morning walk or ride before spending her afternoon hours sketching—via paper or electronic tablet, depending on if she was working for Abby at RoboTech or creating something for her own enjoyment.

The little grassy knoll was her favorite spot, a place where the rolling green hills gave way to a jagged outcropping of rock. The ocean beat against the shore far below, salt-tinged air wafting up the cliffside to tangle her hair and muss the pages of her sketchbook.

God. He couldn't wait to see her.

He'd been in Edinburgh for the past few days, tying up a

few projects before they headed off to winter in the Southern Hemisphere.

Bali, Fiji, New Zealand, and Australia were all on CeCe's travel list.

But before then, he had plans.

And those plans involved Paris and croissants and the Eiffel Tower.

Grinning at the fit she'd throw about not fitting into her jeans because of all the baked goods they would be consuming, Colin headed toward the stables. The wind sliced right through his clothes as he rounded the building, and he decided that spending the coldest part of the year somewhere warm sounded damn good at that moment.

Joanne waved him down as he rode past the front door.

He stopped, bent to take the basket she held up to him. She tsked. "Cecilia didn't take lunch with her."

Colin shook his head, knowing the woman he loved had gotten carried away with sketching again. "I'll make sure she eats."

"Every bite."

A serious nod. "Of course."

Joanne smiled. "You're a good boy, Colin."

He secured the basket then took off at a gallop. Almost a week apart was way too much time.

Her spot appeared in less than twenty minutes, and his breath caught. He shook his head, trying to clear it when all he could concentrate on was CeCe in front of him with long, *long* legs encased in tight denim. Her back was toward him, red curls flying in the breeze, and when she turned to face him, the warmth in her gaze set his heart pounding.

"Hey," she said, once he'd jumped from Bo's back and tied his reins on a nearby log.

She stood, calmly stroking Abharsair's—Devil in English,

Ab for short—neck. Ab had technically been his sister's horse, but he was so ill-tempered—part because of his personality and part because Lana hadn't taken the time to train him properly— that he wouldn't let anyone but CeCe ride him.

Six years ago, she'd tamed the horse with sweet words and a few sugar cubes, and now he was still devoted to Cecilia.

Colin's lips twitched. She managed to inspire that feeling a lot. Joanne, Ab, her friends. Him.

"Hi, sweetheart," he said, coming over and slipping an arm around her waist. Ab tolerated a pat on his forehead before turning away with an expression that bordered on disgust when Colin kissed her.

"I missed you," she said, turning in his arms and hugging him tight.

"Hardly," he teased. "Joanne told me that you've been so busy working and sketching that you haven't eaten."

A guilty expression crossed her face.

"I—"

He tugged her toward Bowen and unstrapped the basket. "I'm to make sure you eat every bite."

She laughed before leading him back over to her blanket and shoving her drawing materials to the side. "With Joanne's cooking, I'm sure that won't be difficult."

He held up a croissant with a smile. "Especially when she packs your favorites?"

She snatched it from his fingers, flopping back onto the blanket and taking a huge bite. Her words were slightly muffed. "I'm going to get fat"—she chewed and swallowed—"And I can't even find the energy to care, not when Joanne makes me home-made croissants every day."

"Careful, you don't choke," he said, lips twitching. "I kind of want to keep you around."

"Meh," she joked. "You'll just find another redhead."

Colin snorted and grabbed an apple from the basket, shifting when CeCe moved to rest her head on his thighs. They stayed like that, eating as they stared out at the cliffs and ocean. Well, *she* was staring at the cliffs and ocean. He was staring at her.

"For the record, I like your spot."

She'd finished the croissant and had closed her eyes. "Hmm?" she asked. Apparently, she'd been doing more dozing than staring.

He bent to press a kiss to her lips.

"Nothing, sweetheart. Go back to sleep." Colin brushed his fingers through her hair, watching as the woman he loved fell asleep on his lap, knowing that they were lucky to have more time together, knowing that he'd cherish every single second—heartfelt or teasing or otherwise.

Knowing that he had the other half of his soul in his arms.

And he wasn't letting her go.

EPILOGUE

Colin, six months later

HE WAS SITTING in the waiting room of a hospital when Cecilia burst through the doors, a huge smile on her face. "It's a girl!"

She launched herself into his arms, kissing him soundly on the mouth. "Abby had a perfect little girl."

Colin stole her lips for another kiss. "How are they?"

"Tired. But healthy and resting." She pushed herself up from his lap. "We should go relieve Bec. She might not *do delivery rooms*, but I'm sure Hunter and Carter are running her ragged."

He smiled, having just spoken with Bec only a half hour before. CeCe's friend *was* being run ragged, but she'd also been in on his plan and enthusiastically *for* it. "I was thinking," he said and held out a gold ring. On it was an obscenely large diamond surrounded by emeralds that matched Cecilia's eyes. "We haven't exactly had the best of luck with planning weddings, so maybe we should go to Vegas instead?"

Her jaw dropped open. "Are you serious?"

A nod.

"I—oh, my God. *Col!*" Tears streaked down her cheeks, but she eventually managed a "yes" and let him slip the ring on her finger.

"How mad do you think your friends will be to miss it?" He nodded in the direction of the door that lead back to where Abby, Jordan, and Seraphina were sequestered.

"Furious." Cecilia grinned. "But I don't care." She threw her arms around his neck and stole another kiss. "We've waited long enough for this, baby. Let's do it."

THE JET WAS ready and waiting, so he just grabbed her hand and led her out to the waiting car.

"Should we stop by the house and pack some clothes?" she asked when they'd buckled in.

Colin pointed to the trunk. "All taken care of."

Cecilia's brows pulled together. "Really? Did you pack me underwear?"

"You doubt me?"

A huff. "How many pairs?"

"Bec packed it for me."

Her face relaxed. "Oh. So, at the hospital, why did you ask—?"

"I didn't want you to miss out on anything you might want." He cupped her cheek and rested his forehead against hers. "After all we've been through, you deserve *everything* you could ever dream of."

"We deserve," she said. "*We* deserve a happily ever after." A beat. "And the only thing I dream of is a future with you. *That's* what's important. Not some silly fantasy, but the fact that I love you with every part of my being."

Her chest was rising and falling in rapid breaths, teasing his lips, and Colin gave in to the urge to kiss her.

He never had any hope of resisting anyway.

Cecilia tasted as sweet as ever, as intoxicating as a bottle of whiskey, and *fuck* did he love kissing this woman.

But eventually, and as much as it pained him, he had to take his hands off her.

"We're here, sir," the driver said with a cough.

CeCe jumped in his arms and pulled back, the tops of her cheeks stained pink.

"You see our need for Vegas," he told the driver then chuckled when CeCe smacked him across the chest. "Come on." He snagged her wrist and tugged her up the stairs to the plane. "Let's get married."

It turned out that though Bec had helped him keep his plan from Cecilia, she hadn't kept it a secret from the rest of their friends.

Case in point, Heather.

Who was standing outside the chapel he'd reserved, phone in hand, and three tiny female faces crammed into the screen on the other side.

"Don't mind me," his business partner said, pointing the phone at them while the interfering hens cackled through the airwaves.

He narrowed his eyes at Bec. "You promised."

An unrepentant shrug. "We'll hang up if you guys really want us to, but we love her and need to see her happy."

"You're nosy," he said.

"That's true." Another shrug. "But also, the other. We want CeCe to be happy."

Sighing, he turned to the woman who would soon be his wife. She was radiantly happy.

"Do you mind?" she asked. "It's kind of perfect that they're here this way."

As if he could ever deny her anything.

He pointed his thumb in the direction of the door. "I guess you ladies are witnessing a wedding."

They squealed as he held open the door for Cecilia and Heather.

"But you'll be witnessing it with the volume on mute."

Heather smirked, adjusting her phone so the noise coming through the speakers wasn't ear-piercing, then twisted her thumb and forefinger in front of her mouth. "My lips are sealed."

He shook his head as his fingers found Cecilia's. "I love you," he whispered, "and can't wait for you to be my wife."

"Awww!" the peanut gallery's sighs were audible despite the low volume on Heather's phone.

Colin rolled his eyes. "Really?"

"Shh, guys," Heather said. "Or you'll get us kicked out."

CeCe gave him a smile that hit him right in the gut. "Let's go grab our happy ending, shall we?"

Thank you for reading! I hope you loved diving into CeCe and Colin's happily ever after! The next book in the Billionaire's Club series is BAD HUSBAND. Find out how what happens when Heather wakes up naked in bed next to her worst enemy... wearing a diamond ring.

CLICK HERE TO READ BAD HUSBAND NOW>

And if you enjoyed BAD BREAKUP, you'll love the small town of Stoneybrooke, its swoony heroes, and the klutzy, lovable heroines who steal their hearts. The first book in the series, TRAIN WRECK, is free to download!

"I laughed out loud all the way through the book, except perhaps during the sexy scenes. I'm not telling you what I did during those." —Amazon reviewer

The more she falls for Stefan, the more she risks her career... Don't miss the Gold Hockey series. It begins with the over 400 five-star-reviewed BLOCKED!

"Off-the-charts hot, smexy scenes with one of the best book boyfriends I have come across!" —Amazon reviewer

DOWNLOAD BLOCKED FOR FREE >

I so appreciate your help in spreading the word about my books, including sharing with friends! Please leave a review on your favorite book site!
You can also join my Facebook group, the Fabinators, for exclusive giveaways and sneak peeks of future books.

SIGN UP FOR ELISE FABER'S NEWSLETTER HERE:
https://www.elisefaber.com/newsletter

Excerpt From BAD HUSBAND

Heather sniffed and swiped a finger under her eyes as Colin and CeCe drove off in their car.

"So, the master businesswoman known as Heather O'Keith

has real human emotions?"

She stiffened, whipping around to glare at Clay Steele, successful businessman, rival entrepreneur, and sexy as fuck male . . . despite the awful porn star name.

"I have plenty of feelings," she snapped. "Just because I don't make a practice of showing them in my fucking boardroom doesn't make me less of a woman."

Clay's stare drifted down and then back up. "Anyone who says you're not a woman has lost their fucking mind."

Heather froze.

Had he—?

Had the man who'd done nothing but dog her steps in the business world, who made it a point of tormenting her by stealing clients and undercutting bids, had *he* just complimented her?

How in the . . .

Then she saw the glassy look in his eyes.

Ah. Drunk.

"You've had a few too many," she said, waving a hand at the town car parked at the corner. Of all the things that came along with busting her ass to have a flush bank account, having enough money to afford a personal driver was a perk that she really enjoyed.

"So?" he asked, not quite belligerent but close.

Idiot men. She'd seen way too many of them in this situation to be the least bit cowed. "I hope you're not an angry drunk."

"No." Both brows came up, waggled. "I'm a horny one."

Despite herself, she chuckled. "With a porn star name like yours, I'm not surprised."

"Hey!" he said and followed her when she strode toward her car, the back door now conveniently open. "I'll have you know, my name is a family one, passed down generation by glorious generation."

A roll of her eyes as she pushed through the open door, plunking down on the plush leather seats. "Maybe so. But you're still drunk."

His expression sobered enough that she stopped short of slamming the metal panel on his head.

Didn't stop her from wanting to do it, though.

His next words made her regret the thought. "Rough day for me today."

Dammit.

Clay seemed to realize he'd said too much and so he stepped back, shoving his hands in his pockets. "Who were they?"

"Friends." *No.* At this point Colin and CeCe were family.

"Ah." One of his hands exited his pocket and shoved through his hair, leaving the thick brown locks mussed. Not that it detracted from the image. Rather, it made Clay Steele appear slightly more human instead of his typical.

Which was godlike.

Tall, broad in the shoulders, lean in the hips, with chocolate-colored hair and unusually vibrant mocha irises.

He'd been in her mental spank bank for months.

"I'd give a lot to have one of those again."

His words made her frown in confusion before she realized she'd spoken aloud. Though thankfully about CeCe and Colin being more than friends and not about her tendency to masturbate to the image of Clay bending her over the bed, pinning her against a wall, grabbing her by the ankles and—

"A family?" she asked, blinking the images away.

"Yeah." A sigh as he turned away. "See you at the next convention, O'Keith."

"Wait!" Acting on an instinct she didn't want to examine too closely, Heather put one foot out of the car, reached to snag his wrist, and hauled him to a stop. "Let me at least take you back to your hotel."

"I'm getting drunk," he said, but allowed her to pull him inside the car so that her driver could shut the door behind them.

"Fine," she said, half-worried he was going to launch himself from the sedan. She'd never seen Clay like this. Usually he was so cold and uncompromising, impenetrable even under the toughest of negotiations. He was . . . well, he was typically as *Steele*-like as his last name decreed.

She grabbed his arm to stop any unplanned exits from the vehicle and gave the driver the name of her favorite bar. "If you want to drink, let's do it right."

And *then* she'd drop him at his hotel.

Except it didn't happen that way.

Yes, they hit the bar.

Yes, they drank.

Yes, they got drunk.

But then they woke up . . . or at least, *Heather* woke up.

Naked.

With a softly snoring Clay Steele passed out next to her in bed.

That wasn't the worst part.

Because Heather woke up naked and with a softly snoring Clay Steele in her bed *and* she was wearing a giant diamond ring on her left hand.

Still not the worst part. *That* came in the form of a slightly crumpled marriage certificate tucked under her right cheek.

And not the one on her face.

She pulled it from beneath her, a cold sweat breaking out on her body, dread in every nerve and cell.

She *still* wasn't prepared for the horror she found.

The marriage license had been signed by . . . Heather O'Keith and Clay Steele.

Holy fuck, what had she done?

Want a free bonus story? Hate missing Elise's new releases?
Love contests, exclusive excerpts and giveaways?
Then signup for Elise's newsletter here!
https://www.elisefaber.com/newsletter

And join Elise's fan group, the Fabinators https://www.
facebook.com/groups/fabinators for insider information, sneak
peaks at new releases, and fun freebies! Hope to see you there!

BILLIONAIRE'S CLUB

Bad Night Stand
Bad Breakup
Bad Husband
Bad Hookup
Bad Divorce
Bad Fiancé
Bad Boyfriend
Bad Blind Date
Bad Wedding
Bad Engagement
Bad Bridesmaid
Bad Swipe
Bad Girlfriend
Bad Best Friend
Bad Billionaire's Quickies

Breakaway

Breakout

Checked

Coasting

Centered

Charging

Caged

Crashed

A Gold Christmas

Cycled

Caught (February 1,2022)

Breakers Hockey (all stand alone)

Broken

Boldly

Breathless

Ballsy (April 26,2022)

Love, Action, Camera (all stand alone)

Dotted Line

Action Shot

Close-Up

End Scene

Meet Cute

Love After Midnight (all stand alone)

Rum And Notes

Virgin Daiquiri

On The Rocks

Sex On The Seats

Life Sucks Series (**all stand alone**)

Train Wreck

Hot Mess

Dumpster Fire

Clusterf*@k

FUBAR (March 29,2022)

Roosevelt Ranch Series (**all stand alone, series complete**)

Disaster at Roosevelt Ranch

Heartbreak at Roosevelt Ranch

Collision at Roosevelt Ranch

Regret at Roosevelt Ranch

Desire at Roosevelt Ranch

Phoenix Series (**read in order**)

Phoenix Rising

Dark Phoenix

Phoenix Freed

Phoenix: LexTal Chronicles (**rereleasing soon, stand alone, Phoenix world**)

From Ashes

In Flames

To Smoke

KTS Series

Riding The Edge

Crossing The Line

Leveling The Field

Scorching The Earth (January 25,2022)

Cocky Heroes World

Tattooed Troublemaker

ABOUT THE AUTHOR

USA Today bestselling author, Elise Faber, loves chocolate, Star Wars, Harry Potter, and hockey (the order depending on the day and how well her team -- the Sharks! -- are playing). She and her husband also play as much hockey as they can squeeze into their schedules, so much so that their typical date night is spent on the ice. Elise changes her hair color more often than some people change their socks, loves sparkly things, and is the mom to two exuberant boys. She lives in Northern California. Connect with her in her Facebook group, the Fabinators or find more information about her books at www.elisefaber.com.

f facebook.com/elisefaberauthor

a amazon.com/author/elisefaber

BB bookbub.com/profile/elise-faber

O instagram.com/elisefaber

g goodreads.com/elisefaber

P pinterest.com/elisefaberwrite